Published in the UK by
Magister Consulting Ltd
The Old Rectory
St Mary's Road
Stone
Dartford
Kent DA9 9AS
UK

Copyright © 2001 Magister Consulting Ltd
First published 2001
Printed in Italy by Fotolito Longo Group

ISBN 1 873839 50 2

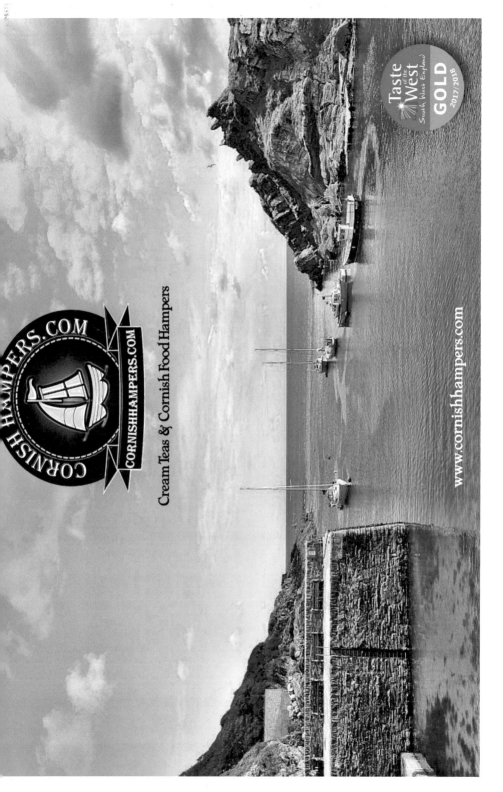

Cream Teas & Cornish Food Hampers

We hope you enjoy your delicious Cornish Hamper brimming with fine, locally sourced Cornish foods. Cornwall is blessed with a rich community of food producers who make their products in small batches from the best local ingredients and we are delighted to be able to share them with you.

- Safe and secure payment
- Personalised gift message
- Over 2,000 Five Star Reviews
- FREE delivery

Delicious Cream Teas and Cornish Food Hampers by Post

My dearest lifelong friend Linda
Hope your feeling better soon
Lots of Love from Pat and Freddie the knicker thief 🥂. xxxx

Cream & scones are at their best when eaten straight away.
Best Before: **17/11/2024**

We hope you enjoy this special treat created just for you!

www.cornishhampers.com |

To Paul
(2002)

Jet,

nearly a labrador, but a true friend
(his life and times)

Introducing

**Storm and Bliss Doberman, Annie Alsatian,
Connie Collie, Lizzie Lurcher, Daisy Dalmation,
Binky Basenji, Polly Poodle and little Minnie Mongrel**

plus

A supporting cast of canines as long as a lurchers tail
(with a horse, a fox, a bull, some sheep,
some chickens and even a few humans)

Tom McGuinn

Let me out!

Let me out of here,

I don't belong in here,

I'm innocent!

Why are humans so stupid; how come they don't understand a word I bark at them. They expect me to understand when they tell me what they want me to do, selfish lot. *'Stop that barking, I'll feed you in a minute'*.

Oh yeah, that's what you said half-an-hour ago and I'm still waiting, so bring the grub pal or get yourself some earplugs. O.K. so that's the way it's going to be in this nick.

Seven days in here and already I'm down as a troublemaker; what's new I ask myself, what's new. Seven weeks old I was, when they wrenched me from the bosom of my family and fostered me out, mind you, mine was a one-parent family and the old mater was beginning to feel the strain of looking after seven youngsters. A bit of all right was my old lady, but she went and got herself mixed up with a no-good tramp of dubious heritage. Labrador she was, black and shiny and a pedigree as long as a wet weekend in Greater Manchester. I suppose if I was a human and not a dog, they would say that I was the product of a broken home, not that I ever clapped eyes on my old fella. Mind you, I wouldn't mind meeting the old reprobate, just out of curiosity you understand.

Jet, nearly a labrador

Hello! I think we're in business; here comes one of the gaolers and I think he's got my dinner with him. *Oh, no!* not punishment rations again. Why can't I have the same as that stuck-up bitch next door. C'mon pal, play the game. Well, beggars can't be choosers so I suppose I'd better get on and eat it or they'll have that vet fella round here shoving pills and capsules down my throttle before you can say 'distemper'. Well, all I can say is if that's dinner, roll on supper.

Six months old and already I've got a criminal record and me as innocent and pure as a newborn Royal Corgi, not that I have any Welsh blood in me, let alone the blue sort. I'll bet those Royal pooches don't have to eat stale meat and rock-hard broken biscuits. 'Man's best friend' my backside. Half a chance, just half a chance and I'll be out of here and back on the streets where I belong. Maybe if I get to be a real pain, they'll just set me free anyway; then again, I could always become a creep like that Staffordshire Bull. He has the cheek to rollover and go all soppy whenever the kennel hands go near him. I wouldn't mind, but I heard him tell his mate the Yorkshire how he used to terrify all the other pets in his neighbourhood. Mind you, the dumb-bells who run this nick don't know anything about all that, they think his owners put him in here because one of them became ill and the other one couldn't look after him properly. The truth is that they both became ill and it was not the usual kind of human sickness, they got sick to death of their neighbours knocking on the door of their house to complain about his chasing their pets. And that's not all. I was told that he got a pedigree poodle pregnant and when her owners threw her out, he deserted her for a border collie. A right hussy by all accounts.

The trouble with most of this lot in here is that they don't know a good thing when they see it. Now take the red setter, a real head-banger if ever I've seen one, but then I suppose that's the Irish in him. He had everything a pup could wish for, big house, massive gardens, the best of grub, a kennel that any cardboard box dweller would be grateful for. Trips out in the family car with the lady of the house and the kids to keep him amused, all that and what does he do? He blows it, that's what.

Quick as the gardener was planting things in the gardens, the wild Colonial Boy was digging them up. Chance after chance he was given, but would he learn, never. You would think that with a pedigree that goes back to Brian Boru he would have enough savvy to know when he was well off. Personally, I blame all that inter-breeding.

If I was to tell you about my first foster home, you wouldn't believe me, but I will tell you anyway. I was a present for a little boy. Well, not so much a little boy, more of a little monster. I could have handled the brat, but the missus, well, she was something else and it was crystal clear that I was not going to get any help from the henpecked hubby. Strangely enough it was her idea to get a pet, or as she put it, a pal for her little darling. They would be company for each other, she told the hubby; what she really meant was that I could keep the brat amused while she spent all morning putting on her war paint and the rest of the day holding court with her cronies. I wouldn't have minded, but the house was only one step up from the council house where I was whelped, and it was mortgaged to the hilt, and then some.

The kid was thoroughly spoilt, but only because the missus couldn't be bothered to put him straight, and a policy of no corporal punishment meant that the brat and his mates - the mini-mafia - got away with murder. Most days the house was like a kindergarten for potential assassins and yours truly was the practice target. Karate chops, head-locks, tail pulling and ear-tweaking were just some of the indignities suffered at the hands of the mini-males, but even worse than that, the female section of the mini-mafia would dress me up in all sorts of kids' clothing, garland my head with ribbons and decorate my legs with bangles, and even garters. I could have put up with all of that if they hadn't taken me out on the streets to play, looking like a fairy. I nearly died the first time it happened when Basher Bates the bull terrier from across the road winked at me, blew me a kiss and asked me what I was doing for the rest of my life. I mean a thing like that can have a lasting affect on one.

Still and all, as far as the digs were concerned, I was quite satisfied. The food was good and there was plenty of it, and although the missus was to cooking what a vet's scalpel is to a tomcat, the quality could not be faulted. There was a clique of women who had food and stuff delivered

Jet, nearly a labrador

to the door; it gave them an air of superiority and the fact that some of them didn't have very much that hadn't been bought on the never-never didn't stop these ladies from playing 'lady of the manor'. Mind you that wasn't all that some of these suburban sirens played at.

Oh boy, could I tell a tale or two about some of the goings-on that us pets get to know about If humans ever get clever enough to communicate properly with us animals, well I dread to think of the consequences.

Take for instance the blonde bit that lived at number seven. About as useful as a chocolate teapot when it came to being a housewife and mother, but I must admit, she looked the business, which was why her old man was willing to put up with her. This pair had a kid that made Rambo seem like Saint Michael the Archangel, all sweetness and light when he was being watched, but when no one was looking he became the creature from hell.

Now twice a week this tiny tyrant was left at our house in the care of my mistress who was not known for her powers of discipline when it came to the mini-mafia. (Mind you, I taught the little horror a thing or two whenever I got the chance.) Now, the blond bombshell had talked her ever-loving into buying her a horse that she could learn to ride, which explains the twice a week dumping of her brat on our household. Now I'm not one to gossip, but when our family was invited to go along to the stables to meet 'Flashy' I found out things that a pup of barely seven months shouldn't ever know. Flashy the horse was all that his name suggested. A golden chestnut with a lot of white about him and full of himself. In fact, the blonde bimbo and Flashy made a right pair of you know-what's.

It was when the yuppies went into the Lodge for morning coffee that I managed to have a quiet word with old Flashy and what he told me made my hair stand on end. Apparently Flashy was no more than an excuse for the bimbo and the head groom to get together twice a week and not just for riding lessons either. On the way home from the stables the bimbo said that as she was getting on so well with the lessons she was thinking of going three times a week and would it be all right to leave the infamous infant with us for the extra day?. It was when my dozy mistress agreed that I decided enough was enough, so I planned to have it on my toes, or in my case, paws. It was going to be hell-on-earth when the bimbo's ever-loving discovered what was going on, and our lord and master could never be convinced that his other half was totally oblivious of the ever increasing romps in the straw, and after all, weren't the bimbo's ever-loving and our lord and master bosom buddies. In fact, Dinky the Dachshund, whose master is a member of the local Masons Lodge told me that he had seen all three of them with one trouser leg turned up while making funny signs at each other.

One-by-one I waited for an opportunity to say goodbye to my mates, Basher Bates the Bull Terrier, Dinky the Dachshund, Polly the Poodle, Tyson the Boxer (after Mike) and Lizzie the Lurcher, who incidentally I had a real crush on, but as time proved, it was only puppy love. I had to wait for the right opportunity and I didn't have too long to wait. It happened one day when the bimbo's brat was at our house and he was being more horrible than usual. For him, that put his behaviour in the same league as Damien-the-Devil-Child on a bad day. Being a Labrador, well, nearly a Labrador, I was expected to take anything and everything that was dished out to me, so you can imagine the uproar when I bared my teeth and gave the child-from-hell the fright of his life. Rumour had it that the little lout was never ever cruel to any animal ever again.

Anyway, I had it away and I knew exactly where I was heading for. Lizzie the Lurcher told me of some private boarding kennels in the countryside where she goes when her owners go abroad. Lizzie said that there were guard dogs running loose within the confines of the kennel and if I mentioned her name the two guard dogs would let me in under the wire fence.

Sure enough when I eventually reached the boarding kennels late that evening, there they were, the most frightening sight I had ever seen in my life, two Dobermans; Blizzard a bitch, and her brother Storm. Lizzie had told me that Blizzard and Storm had been trained especially for the job, which meant that they could guard the place without

barking for fear of waking up the guests. I found out what Lizzie
meant when I sidled up to the wire fence only to be met by Storm,
teeth stripped and looking more menacing than a bear with a sore head.

"What do you want, scruffy", asked Storm through his gritted teeth.

"Are you called Storm," I asked, "and have you got a sister called
Blizzard".

"That's right," said Storm, "What's it to you?" By that time, Blizzard
had arrived to stand beside her brother.

"Who is this?" she asked, "and what does the little mongrel want".

"Please Miss," I said, "I need somewhere to hide out for a few days
and Lizzie Lurcher said that you would help me".

"Where did a scraggy little rogue like you get to meet Lizzie?"

I told them my story, and as I was a friend of Lizzie's, they agreed to
help. Storm showed me the spot where I could crawl under the wire
fence. When I was inside, they took me around the kennels and
introduced me to the paying guests. As it was not yet the holiday season,

there were only four guests; Boris the Borzoi, Alzah the Afghan and the two Yorkshires: Spick and Span.

"Are you very hungry?" asked Spick.

"Of course he's hungry" said Span, "you'd be hungry if you'd been on the run".

"Do you really know Lizzie Lurcher?" asked Boris, "only our owners usually go to America for their summer holidays and Lizzie and I come here".

"Alright, alright", said Storm, "let's break it up now and find something for this young rascal to eat".

"What's your name?" asked Blizzard. "I suppose you do have a name". "Labby" I replied.

"Labby" shrieked Blizzard. "What sort of name is that?" at which point they all had a good old giggle.

"Who in heavens name christened you that, and why for God's sake" asked Alzah the Afghan.

"I think the missus gave me that name because I'm a Labrador".

"You are not a Labrador" said Storm "and the sooner you admit that to yourself the better, or you're going to get into more trouble than you can handle".

"My mum was a Labrador, and I take after her," I said.

"Now, now" said Blizzard, "we'll talk about that in the morning. In the meantime let's find somewhere for you to sleep".

"Remember" said Storm, "you must not go walking about unless Bliss" (his name for his sister) "or I give you the all-clear". As I was walking away, Boris said that they would have a late night meeting to decide on a new name for me. I had a good meal and I slept like a log.

Early the next morning Bliss came to see me and to explain what I had to do so as not to be discovered by the kennel staff. Bliss said that

Jet, nearly a labrador

as it was the slack time of the year, there was very little chance of that as there was only the manager and his wife and neither of them were over fond of work.

"Mind you" said Bliss "that's not to say that the guests don't get properly looked after, because they do. It's just that at this time of year there is not so much pampering going on".

"Now" said Bliss, "this place where you are now is where the fresh bedding (straw) is stored, and once the staff have taken out what they need for the day, they will not come in again until the next morning". She went on to explain that the bedding was changed by some of the staff as others saw to the meals. As the kennel manager and his wife were performing those duties at present, it would be easy to keep tabs on them, and let me know when to make myself scarce until they had finished. There would be other times throughout the day when the manager would visit the kennels, about four times in all, so Bliss and Storm had arranged with the guests that Boris the Borzoi should be the one they would rely on to raise the alarm that the manager was on his way to the kennels. The manager had to pass Boris's quarters to get to the bedding store and as Boris could bark loudest, he was the obvious choice.

"When you hear Boris's signal" Bliss explained, "you must leave the area, go to the spot where we let you in last night; Storm will be waiting to let you through the fence and you can go and visit the town for a couple of hours". Bliss explained that it would only be during the mornings that I would actually have to leave the compound, as it would be then when the manager would visit the bedding store. Bliss told me that if I did go to town I must not go right into the centre. She told me of a friend who lived at a restaurant on the outskirts. This friend, Annie the Alsatian, usually spent her holidays at the kennels and if I told Annie that she, Bliss, had sent me, then I would be made welcome. "Tell Annie your story and tell her that you are staying with Storm and me at Three-Tops (so called because of the three huge oaks in the middle of the compound) and give her our love".

Bliss told me that when the holiday season was in full swing and there was extra staff on duty, the manager and his wife liked to visit Annie's restaurant and have a meal in the beautiful gardens in which the place stood. Bliss and Storm went too, a kind of treat and a break from their duties as guardians of Three-Tops, and its pampered guests. Annie's restaurant was somewhere that owners took their dogs and as Bliss and Storm went there once a week it gave them a chance to meet old friends and talk about who was in residence at Three-Tops. It was also very handy for Bliss and Storm to pass on messages to their many friends in the area. They would give the message to Annie and well, what Annie the Alsatian didn't know about local gossip, just wasn't worth knowing. "Now I wouldn't say that Annie herself was a gossip," said Bliss, "but if the whole of the County don't know that you are staying with us within a couple of days, then I'm a Pekinese".

It was some time later when I heard Boris sounding the alarm to let me know that the manager had just left his house, and was about to start the morning duties. I peeped outside to make sure the coast was clear, then I made my way to the spot where I knew Storm would be waiting for me. When I got to the bit of fence with the secret door-way hidden by a large bush, Storm was waiting for me.

"Now remember" said Storm "stay off the roads, it's quite easy to get to Annie's place by going across country". Storm gave me directions and said that if I stuck to the route I would come across the little house where Connie the Collie lived with her master old Sean the shepherd. "If you meet Connie, tell her that we were asking for her and give her our best wishes and whatever you do, stay well away from the sheep, otherwise Sean the shepherd will be after you".

It was a nice bright spring morning as I made my way through the fields and woods, the sun was shining and I felt really happy to be free. No tail pulling, no ear tweaking and lots of new friends, no wonder I was feeling happy. A little stream by the side of a wood looked so clear and bright that I just had to have a drink from it. The water tasted lovely and a paddle in the little stream was more than welcome to my paws. It was while I was having a paddle that the big Collie rushed out of the wood and scared the living daylights out of me. Before I had a chance to utter a word, I was on my back with the Collie glaring down on me.

Jet, nearly a labrador

"Who are you and what are you doing on this land, don't you know anything; unaccompanied dogs are not allowed where there are sheep or other livestock. Is there a human with you? Why aren't you on a lead; where did you come from and where are you going?" The surprise attack and then the flood of questions had my head swimming and I couldn't get a word out of my mouth, but even so, all the time I was hoping that the big frame that I was staring up at belonged to Connie. "Speak up young fella or I will take you to my master, he'll know what to do with you. Tell the truth now, have you been chasing my sheep?"

"No, no" I managed to blurt out. "I am on my way to visit Annie at the Freshwater Restaurant. Is your name Connie?" I asked meekly.

"Yes" answered the big Collie, "but how do you know my name?"

"Blizzard and Storm from Three-Tops told me that I might meet you on the way to Annie's".

"Are you a run-away from Three-Tops?" asked Connie. I told my story to Connie, and told her that Blizzard and Storm sent their best wishes and could I please stand up now as the water was freezing my bones. "I am sorry" said Connie "only you can't be too careful when you have all these sheep to look after and, well, you could have been one of those townies who chase my sheep all over the County".

"Oh no" I said, "I wouldn't do a thing like that, I'm a Labrador".

"Who told you that you are a Labrador?" said Connie, "you don't look all Labrador to me".

"My mum was a Labrador and I take after her," I said.

"Silly boy" said Connie tiresomely. "Did you ever see your father?" she asked.

"No" I answered, "and my mum never talked about him".

"Now you listen to me my lad" said Connie sternly, "if you are ever going to make anything of yourself, you must first learn to be yourself and not something you are not. Right" said Connie "I have work to do so you'd better be on your way. Now, if you want a bit of advice, you will do well to keep to the little stream, it's the longest way round to Annie's, but it does run past the restaurant gardens, so at least you won't get lost. By the way" said Connie, "Will you be coming back this way tonight, or are you staying over with Annie?"

"I'll be coming back," I said. "I'm staying at Three-Tops for a while".

"Well in that case, remember to keep to the stream, and whatever you do, don't disturb my sheep and tell Annie that I hope to see her Saturday when old Sean treats himself to his weekly slap-up, as he calls it. Off you go then" said Connie "Off you go, I have better things to do than to pass the time of day with someone who thinks he's a Labrador when he's not".

"I don't care what you say, I am a Labrador," I said under my breath, and well out of earshot, as I made a start on the rest of my journey to the Freshwater Restaurant and the well-known Annie.

I took Connie's advice and never strayed far from the little stream, although the little stream wasn't so little in some places and I even saw some fishermen sitting on the side and talking to each other. Just as

Jet, nearly a labrador

Connie had said, the stream brought me to the bottom of the restaurant gardens. I could see the restaurant through the trees and there was no fence so I went very carefully towards what looked like a kennel. The kennel was empty and there was no sign of Annie; there was no sign of life anywhere. I suppose I am in the right place I thought, as I looked around the gardens. Oh dear I thought, I wish I could read. I know what I will do; I will go around to the front. Maybe there's a clue that will tell me if I'm in the right place. There was a big sign, it had a picture of a river and you could see the fish swimming in it. I am in the right place I thought as I decided that the picture was where the name Clearwater came from. I was still telling myself what a clever Labrador I was, when I was almost run over by the Range Rover turning into the driveway. I was behind the bushes in a flash and waited to see who got out of the Rover. A man got out of the driver's side and hot on his heels came the welcome sight of an Alsatian, which I hoped and prayed would be Annie. Sure enough it was Annie because the man shouted at her.

"Annie, what have I told you? you must wait where you are until I let you out your side". Annie looked at the man and she gave him that 'please-don't-shout-at-me glance' that my mum said bitches do so well. The poor man was melted instantly; he bent down and said ever so softly, "now then old girl, I have to tell you these things to stop you hurting yourself". Well, I thought, she has him well and truly where she wants him. The man took a box of something from the back of the Rover and took it into the restaurant; Annie followed him. Oh dear, I thought, I'll never get to talk to her. The man returned and he had a lady with him. They both took some more boxes from the car. But where was Annie? When the two people had gone back inside I moved nearer to see if I could find out where Annie was. I could see through the glass door, and what I saw made me wonder if I would ever get to talk to Annie today. Annie was curled up on a huge settee and I was sure that I could hear her snoring. I couldn't stay out in the open for fear of being captured and taken back to my home, which had become such an unhappy place for me. There was only one thing for it; I would wait in Annie's kennel. What a lovely kennel it was and ever so comfortable, so comfortable that I fell asleep and the next thing I knew I was once again being straddled by a huge dog asking questions.

"Who are you, what are you doing in my kennel, where did you come from?" The next question was the one I could answer the quickest. "Who said you could come into my garden?"

Quick as I could, I blurted out "Blizzard, Storm, Three-Tops".

"Have you got a message for me then?"

"Not from Three-Tops" I said, "but Connie said to tell you that she will see you on Saturday".

"Oh do try to make sense you silly little boy," said Annie. "What has

Jet, nearly a labrador

Connie got to do with Three-Tops and what about Blizzard and Storm? I'll tell you what" said Annie, "suppose you start at the beginning and tell me all about why you are here".

After I told Annie my story, she said that she understood because when she was young, she once ran away from a place where she was very unhappy.

"Are you hungry?" asked Annie.

"I'm starving," I answered.

"Well" said Annie, "my master will be bringing some food out to me very shortly. He always makes me up a snack from whatever they are cooking for the lunchtime menu".

"But, I can't eat your food" I said, hoping of course that Annie would win the argument, which wasn't going to be difficult as I was not going to resist her offer very much.

"Now, now", said Annie, "I will hear no more about it, you are too young to be going hungry and God only knows what Blizzard would say if I didn't look after you properly, and besides, it's about time I did something about my figure before the tourist season begins".

"Do you live outside all the time?" I asked Annie.

"Oh no," she answered, "I live in the house during the winter."

"Which do you prefer", I asked, "Indoors or outdoors?"

"Well" said Annie, "It is lovely to be all snug and cosy when the rain and sleet of winter is lashing against the windows, but it is equally lovely to be outside when it is very, very hot indoors, so I get the best of both worlds. I can't really choose. Ssshh, someone's coming, move to the back of the kennel and I'll go out to meet whoever it is." It was Annie's master with her snack.

"Here you are old girl," I heard him say; "I think you are going to like this". The master put the snack down outside the kennel and went back inside. Annie popped her head into the kennel and said, "Come on young man, come and have some food, and when you have eaten, we can go down by the stream". I suggested to Annie that we share the food, but she insisted that I eat it all, saying that she could have all the food she could eat anytime. After I had done justice to the most beautiful snack I had ever eaten in my life, Annie took me on a tour of the gardens, which were massive. One section was an orchard, another was for the fresh vegetables for the restaurant and Annie told me that one of her duties was to prevent the birds and rabbits from gobbling up all the young plants. "Tell me, how are Storm and Bliss?" enquired Annie. "Are there many guests at Three-Tops at the moment?"

"They are both very well" I told her, and there were only four guests in residence at the moment. Annie told me how she looked forward to her stays at Three-Tops and especially the late night story telling. When we reached the stream, Annie asked me what I wanted to be when I was older, I said I didn't know, but as I was a Labrador, I would do what Labradors do.

"Come now," said Annie, "Surely you don't believe that you are all Labrador; has nobody told you then, your mother may well have been a Labrador, but did you ever meet your father?" We sat on the bank beside the stream and Annie told me the very same things that all the others had told me. "You are what you are" Annie told me, "and telling people you are something else will just get you laughed at. By the way, what is your name?" asked Annie.

"Labby" I answered.

"Labby" shrieked Annie, just as Blizzard had done. "Oh my dear, do forgive me laughing, but that will have to be changed and no mistake". It was then that I told myself that they could not all be wrong.

"But I do look like a Labrador" I insisted.

"Indeed you do" said Annie, "and you would surely pass as a Labrador to many, but to those who know better, hardly. You are a very handsome young fellow and it is obvious from what you tell me, that you do indeed take after your mother, which is a very good reason for

Jet, nearly a labrador

making her proud of you." I told Annie what Storm and Bliss had said about changing my name and she said that I would do well to listen to them as they were very, very intelligent. "You must never be ashamed of your mother just because she fell for someone different from herself, because I'm sure your Mum would never be ashamed of you."

"Have you had a family?" I asked.

"Yes I have" replied Annie "and I too, like your mother, fell for a rascal not of my own kind".

"Where are they now" I asked.

"As far as I know, when they left me, they were all taken to be trained for Air Force Police duties".

"Were you very unhappy when your family were taken from you?"

"Yes I was" said Annie, "and it was made so much worse when even some of my best friends turned against me for bringing shame on our strictly pedigree kennels, so I left".

"Where did you go?" I asked.

"Well" said Annie, "Unlike you I didn't know anyone outside our kennels, and I just knew that I had to keep going until I was so far away that they would never find me".

"How did you come to be living here?" I asked her.

"Well now" said Annie, "I will tell you; I had been on the road for about a week and living on whatever scraps I could find. I was all worn out, and couldn't go very much further when I came upon a little house in the middle of nowhere. At the side of the little house there was a little shed, and on the floor of the shed was a bed of straw. It was very late at night and as there was nobody about I decided to have a rest. I was so tired that I'm sure I was asleep before I laid my poor weary body down. I didn't know how long I had been asleep, but when I came to my senses, the first thing I realised was that the door of the shed was closed and locked from the outside. I didn't panic. I think I was still far too tired and sore to even worry about it. I didn't have long to wait for whatever fate had in store for me. I heard the bolt being pulled back and I moved to the back of the shed not knowing what was about to come through the door. The door opened and as it did, a man's voice said *"It's all right my dear, there is no need to worry, sure now I'm not going to hurt nor harm ye"*. Behind the man was a Collie who looked like I felt. In fact it was hard to know which of the three of us was the most frightened. The man moved towards me and somehow found enough courage to reach out to me. Something about the man told me that there was nothing to be scared about; his voice was soft and warm and there was kindness in his face. I moved as to meet him halfway in trust as well as distance and his weather-beaten hand fell gently on my brow as he reassured me. By this time the cowardly Collie had picked up enough courage to venture into the shed and that was how I came to meet Connie the Collie and old Sean the Shepherd. I was with him for about a week when Sean brought a man to see me. The man had told Sean that he and his wife had decided to find a nice pet to live at their restaurant and that's how I came to be living here".

"You were ever so lucky," I said.

Jet, nearly a labrador

"Yes, I know," said Annie. "You don't want to leave it too late before you start back to Three-Tops, unless of course you want to stay here tonight? You're very welcome". I told Annie that I would like to stay, but they made me promise not to as they would only worry about me at Three-Tops. "Do you want to come here tomorrow?" asked Annie.

"Yes please," I answered.

"Right you are" said Annie, "Tell Bliss that you can come here whenever you want to as long as it is alright with her. Now you be very careful on the way back, and whatever you do, don't disturb Connie's sheep; tell Bliss and Storm that we will have to arrange a late night meeting to decide what to do about you, and in the meantime, they are to help you pick a new name - Labby indeed. Off with you now or it will be dark before you get back".

I was feeling really good as I made my way back and I couldn't help thinking back to yesterday morning and how alone and frightened I had felt before I had found my way to Three-Tops. As I passed through Connie's area I was ever so careful not to disturb her sheep. It was almost dark when I arrived back, and Storm was waiting by the secret entrance. "Have you been waiting long?" I asked. "No, no" said Storm, and anyway I have to patrol the fence-line every half-hour during daylight and I am on my last round so you could not have timed it better. "Come" said Storm, "we have all saved you some of our food; you must eat first then you can tell us all about your day. Follow me," said Storm as he led the way through the bushes towards the bedding store. When we were inside the store, Storm explained that there was to be a meeting later that night when the manager and his wife had gone to bed. Everyone was to meet in the bedding store to decide what was to become of me.

Much later, Bliss came into the storeroom and said that the others would be along shortly. When everyone had arrived, Bliss asked me to tell all about my day - had I met Connie and what did I think of her? How did I get on at the Freshwater Restaurant and did Annie tell me all about how she had met old Sean the Shepherd and Connie? According to Bliss, Annie's life story was well known by everyone who ever visited the Freshwater Restaurant. They asked if I was going back there tomorrow. I said that I would like to if it was all right with them. Spick and Span asked what I had to eat at Annie's; Boris wanted to know if I had helped Connie with her sheep, while Alzah said that as I was going to Annie's tomorrow, would I tell her that he was asking after her. When all the curiosity had been satisfied, Bliss said that the first thing we should do was find a new name for me,

"Something less stupid than *Labby*," said Storm. "I do beg your pardon," he said "I know its not your fault that you were given such a soppy name."

"I know," said Boris, "let's all have one suggestion each and if we can't agree on one of those names, we can have a second suggestion and so on until we find one that we all like; him too" he added, looking at me.

"Alright, agreed," said Bliss, "But the name we choose must have some meaning".

"What do you mean?" asked Spick.

"Well" said Bliss, "For instance, my brother and I were born one night during the winter when the weather was very bad and because of that, our owners named us after things to do with the weather, hence Storm and Blizzard".

"Did you have brothers and sisters?" asked Span."

"Yes we did," answered Storm. "We had two brothers and two sisters."

"What were their names?" I asked.

"Well," said Bliss, "the boys were called Tempest and Thunder and of course Storm and the girls were called Gale and Breeze and of course Blizzard."

"What lovely names your family have," said Alzah. "I wish I had been born in a storm then I could have had a nice name with a meaning."

"I wonder why our owners called us Spick and Span?" asked Spick.

"Don't you know?" said Bliss. "I do, I overheard the kennel manager telling his wife that your owners thought that you looked the cleanest

Jet, nearly a labrador

most tidy dogs they had ever seen in their lives so they decided to give you meaningful names" Bliss told Alzah that she was sure that his name had a special meaning too.

"What about my name?" asked Boris "Do you think my name is meaningful?"

"Oh yes indeed," said Storm. "Boris is a very strong name and as you are of Russian descent it suits you well, and it's a constant reminder of your heritage.'

"Now then," said Boris "who would like to go first to suggest a new name for Labby?" The guests all answered at the same time.

"Me first," said Spick.

"No," said Span, "me first."

"No, no," said Boris "I'll go first."

"We'll go in alphabetical order," said Alzah. "So it's my turn first, then

Boris, then, oh dear, who shall go first between those two?" she looked at Spick and Span. Storm said that as both their names began with the same letter we would have to have a vote, a vote to decide which one went first.

"Nonsense," said Blizzard, "you're beginning to sound like your owners; Spick will go first because she is a girl and even humans agree that it's always ladies before gentlemen".

"Now that's settled, can we please make a start," said Storm "What's-his-name", meaning me, "has had a very busy day and he should have an early night so that he can catch up with his sleep".

"What about Rover?", said Alzah.

"Well it's a start," said Bliss who had taken complete charge of the proceedings, as indeed she always did. "But Rover is so old-fashioned and anyway it would make him sound like a car".

"How does Piper sound?" said Boris. "I once knew a Scots Terrier called Piper and he loved his name."

"Well be that as it may, and Piper is a really lovely name for a Scots Terrier," said Storm, "but our little friend is far from being a Scots Terrier."

"I know," said Spick, "we will give him a name with some meaning and as Labradors usually work for people who use guns, we could call him Rifle."

"Now I like that name," I said. "Can I have that one?"

"Silly boy," said Bliss "How many times need you be told that you are not all Labrador and shame on you Spick for encouraging him, you ought to know better. However, Rifle would indeed be a wonderful name for a gundog and if we ever have to re-name a runaway work-ing dog then Rifle will be top of our list of names."

"What about you Span, have you got a name for him?" asked Bliss.

"Yes I have," Span answered "And I think it is a name with real meaning."

Jet, nearly a labrador

"Oh come on then," said everyone in chorus, "Let us hear it."

"Tramp!" said Span, "Let's call him Tramp! After all, he is a kind of Tramp at the moment."

"Very good," said Storm, "But he won't be a Tramp forever, at least we hope not."

"That's very meaningful," said Bliss sarcastically. "I'm just very glad that you didn't name us. Storm might now be called Hailstone and I might be called Snowflake." Name after name was suggested, but somehow none of then seemed very suitable; Bruce, Toby, Prince, Duke and dozens more. I was beginning to feel like Mr. Nobody when Bliss said "How about Soot, that's meaningful as he is as black as a chimney."

"Not bad," said Storm, "but I don't think that is a very dignified name for someone who is nearly a Labrador, even if he is black all over."

"I know," said Boris "let's call him 'Jet' because he's jet black."

"Oh good," agreed Alzah, "that's a wonderful name."

"What do you think?" asked Storm, turning to me "After all, it is going to be your name." I said I liked it much better than Labby as I thought how much Jet sounded like a Labrador.

"That's settled then," said Bliss. "It's very late, so we will have to go to bed now; we can talk again about what to do about Jet's future." I felt good as I lay down and I was still thinking about my new name as I dropped off to sleep.

Next morning Bliss woke me up and I thought it was very funny when she called me by my new name. "Wakey, wakey, good morning, Jet," said Bliss as she urged me to hurry up as we had all overslept due to being up so late the night before. "It's a beautiful morning" said Bliss. "And if you leave now you will have time enough to stop by and see Connie. Perhaps if you ask her nicely, she will let you help with her sheep."

Just as I was leaving, Storm appeared and asked Bliss if I should tell Connie and Annie that there would be a little get together Friday night at Three-Tops. It didn't take me very long to get to Connie's and I was very excited at the thought of helping Connie with her sheep.

"Good morning Connie".

"Good morning Labby" said Connie as we met near the stream.

"My name is not Labby any longer, my new name is *Jet*," I said proudly.

"Oh well" said Connie, "now that is a proper name for someone who is nearly a Labrador."

"Can I help you?" I asked.

"Yes," said Connie, "but you must be very gentle with the sheep because this is the time of year when the lambs are born. As you will see, there are lots of babies with their mums and there are still some mums yet to have their babies."

"What shall I do to help?" I asked.

"We can move the flock from the low ground to the higher fields where the grass is fresher from the morning dew. Go very steady now," said Connie "or you will scare them, they won't be so nervous when they get to know you. We worked very hard coaxing the flock to the sweeter grass and when we had done, Connie said that I had been a great help to her. "Let's go down to the stream for a drink and a paddle," said Connie, "The sheep will not want to stray from this lovely grazing."

Jet, nearly a labrador

On the way to the stream I told Connie about the get-together at Three-Tops on Friday night. She said to tell Bliss that she would love to go and she would be along as soon as the flock settled for the night. We reached the stream and the cool water was so inviting, I drank so much that Connie said I would pop. When we had drunk, paddled and rested, Connie said that I should make my way to Freshwater as Annie would be worried if I was very late arriving.

When I reached Freshwater, Annie was waiting at the bottom of the gardens. She said that she had been so concerned that she was about to go off in search of me. I told Annie that I had been helping Connie with her sheep and I was sorry if I had upset her.

"It's alright," said Annie, "now that I know you are safe. Did you enjoy helping Connie with her sheep?"

"Oh yes," I answered. "It was ever so exciting and Connie is clever and so gentle and kind to the sheep, especially the mother sheep and their new babies."

"Well" said Annie, "Connie does come from a long line of sheep carers; she may well be gentle with her sheep, but woe betide anyone who would be silly enough to harm or upset one of her lambs." I remembered how Connie had crept up on me the first time we met and how frightening she looked as she pinned me to the bed of the stream, so I could imagine how tough she could be if necessary.

Annie asked me if I would like to hear the story of Connie and the missing lamb. "Yes please," I said. "Come then" said Connie, "Let's make ourselves comfortable in my kennel."

Before Annie told her story, I told her of the get-together at Three-Tops on Friday night and how we stayed up late last night deciding on a new name for me. 'Jet', I told her was my new name. "Do you like it?" I asked. "It's a very fitting name for someone who is nearly a Labrador and black all over," said Annie.

It was when Connie was very young that the saga of the missing lamb took place. Connie had arrived at Sean the shepherd's little house as a surprise present and a replacement for Sally who was getting near the time when she could retire and take things easy. Although Connie had been born on a sheep farm and her family had been sheep dogs for many, many generations, she would still need to be taught many things by Sean before she could take over the flock from the faithful Sally. Connie was a willing pupil and was soon doing so much work that Sally was able to take things easy even before her time came to retire.

Sean had been worried that Sally might be sad to see someone younger doing her job, but when he saw how Sally mothered Connie, he knew that his fears were unfounded. It was not only Sean that Connie was learning from, but Sally was teaching her some tricks of their trade, that not even a great shepherd like Sean could teach her.

Connie was barely one year old and Sally was about to retire when the travelling people from all over the country gathered for the annual horse fair. Although it was called a horse fair you could buy, sell or trade just about anything. Sean the shepherd always looked forward to the fair as he had many friends amongst the travellers. Some of the families were allowed to make camp on Sean's land, but they would be the real horse traders whose ancestors had been coming to the fair for generations and they knew how to behave in the country and especially around livestock. However, it was unfortunate that as well as the well-behaved travellers, there were always one or two families who found it difficult to get through the three day fair without causing some upset or other. The fair was also a target for some mischief-making townies who just had no respect for the countryside. The fair was a time for being more alert than ever for people like Sean, and as for sheep dogs, well they scarcely got any rest at all.

Anyway, although Sally had only a matter of days to go before her retirement, she told Connie that she would do her full share of the work in protecting the flock whilst the fair was on. Normally Sean would borrow another sheep dog to help Sally during those three days, but having Connie to help this year, he was sure they could manage. Although Sean, Sally and Connie worked tirelessly to keep unruly dogs and even more unruly humans away from the flock, the morning after the fair had moved on, Connie came across a ewe searching everywhere for her missing lamb. Connie was very upset and was blaming herself for not protecting the lamb, but Sally told her that it was not the first lamb to have gone missing. Connie overheard Sean telling his friend that an unscrupulous traveller probably stole the lamb. No matter how she tried, Sally could not console Connie, and when Connie asked Sally if she would look after the flock, she knew that her young friend was going in search of the missing lamb.

After a full day and no sign of Connie, Sean reported her missing to the police. It was four days later when Police Constable Larry Law called at Sean's house to tell him that a Collie answering Connie's description was being held at a police station almost forty miles away and would he go there as the police were quite certain that it was Connie. "How can they be so sure?" asked Sean.

"Well," said Constable Law, "when she was found, she was very much the worse for wear, but she still insisted on protecting the lamb she had with her".

"That is the best story I have ever heard," I told Annie, "but how did Connie get the lamb back and who had stolen the lamb?"

"Well now," said Annie, "that is still a mystery because Connie has never ever told even Sally. All we know is that Connie told a friend that she found the lamb wandering near a traveller's camp-site".

Annie had just finished telling me about Connie and the missing lamb, when we heard her owner calling snack time. He called "come and get it".

"Oh dear," said Annie, "If I go up to the restaurant he will wait while I eat the snack and I won't be able to share it with you. I know, you go hide and I'll pretend to be asleep, then he will bring the snack down here and leave it outside the kennel.

"Come on old girl," called her owner, but Annie kept as quiet as a mouse.

Eventually the snack was brought to the kennel and for a moment I thought I heard Annie chuckling. When we had eaten the snack, Annie said that she would have to pay a visit to the vegetable garden to make sure that there were no rabbits or birds gobbling up all the plants.

"Can I come?" I asked. "I'll be ever so quiet".

"Yes you can come, but it doesn't matter if you make a little noise, all I want to do is scare them off".

"Do you have to scare them off every day?" I asked.

"Oh my dear", said Annie, "I have to chase them off every hour some days".

"But won't they starve if everyone stops them from eating?"

"Oh no, there are plenty of other things to eat in the countryside at this time of the year. Besides, we have only got a very small vegetable garden compared to the farms and if we didn't chase them off they would soon make all our plants disappear".

Jet, nearly a labrador

When we had chased the birds and the rabbits out of the vegetable garden, we went for a paddle in the stream. Annie said that whenever she had a paddle in the stream, she would think about her friends.

"Why?" I asked.

"Well", said Annie, "the stream runs past the bottom of Three-Tops' gardens and it also runs through old Sean's land and I'm sure that there are some days when Storm, Bliss, Sally, Connie and myself are all having a paddle at the same time. At least, that's what I imagine and that's what makes me think of them".

We spent the afternoon talking and keeping the birds and rabbits out of the vegetable garden.

Annie said I was a lucky young fella to have the chance to learn so many things at Three-Tops. "You can learn all about patrolling and guarding property; at old Sean's you can learn all about looking after a flock of sheep and here at Freshwater you can learn all about protecting a vegetable garden".

As I left Freshwater to make my way back to Three-Tops, Annie told me to tell Storm and Bliss that she would be coming to the get together tomorrow night for certain. As I had to pass through old Sean's land I thought I would call and remind Connie about tomorrow night. When I got to Connie's she was having a paddle in the stream and that reminded me of what Annie had said and I understood what she meant about a paddle in the stream reminding her of her friends.

Connie told me that she had been very busy and her feet were killing her.

"I haven't forgotten," she said. "I'll be there for certain".

I said goodbye to Connie and made my way to Three-Tops. I waited at the secret entrance and before very long Storm came along.

"You'll never guess who's come to stay," he said. I said that I had no idea. "Lizzie, you know, Lizzie Lurcher and she's been asking all about you. She said that she had been very worried about you and had you found Three-Tops before anything bad happened to you? Come, let's get you to the bedding store before you're discovered".

Bliss was waiting in the store to tell me that I must not make any noise this evening. She explained that when a new guest arrived the kennel manager or someone would check every so often to make sure that they were settling in all right. "But Lizzie has been here before," I said. "That's right," said Bliss, "but they still make sure, so remember, quiet as a mouse. We'll let you talk to Lizzie when it's safe to do so."

Later that evening Bliss took me to see Lizzie while Storm kept watch on the manager's house, in case he decided to visit the kennels. "Oh it is good to see you," said Lizzie, "I was so worried about you when you left home. Polly Poodle told me that she had heard a rumour that you had been dog-napped by some travellers". Bliss said that Lizzie Lurcher should know better than to believe anything that Polly Poodle said, besides, all Polly's family were given to fantasising.

"Tell me about the others," I asked.

"Well now," said Lizzie, "Basher Bates the Bull Terrier and Tyson the Boxer had been grounded for going into town and getting into a fight with the townies; Dinky Dachshund had been to London to see the Queen and now she pretends that she is a Royal Corgi".

Jet, nearly a labrador

"Do you miss your home?" Lizzie asked me.

"Oh no, not at all," I replied. "I'm having a wonderful time and I am learning lots and lots of things for when I find a new owner".

"That's good," said Lizzie, "especially if you find an owner who likes the countryside.

After a while Bliss said that we should all have an early night as we were having a get-together tomorrow night, and that usually meant hardly any sleep at all. I went to bed, but I was so excited about the get-together that I hardly slept, even though I had had such a busy day.

"Good morning Jet," said Bliss as she tried to wake me up, but I was so tired that I asked her if I could have a lie-in. "Oh now," said Bliss, "I will have to see what Storm thinks". Bliss went to find Storm and I went back to sleep. They didn't wake me again until the very last minute before someone might come into the store. When they did wake me, Bliss said that it might be a good idea if I stayed around Three-Tops today. "We will just have to do our best to make sure you are not discovered. Anyway Storm overheard the manager telling his wife that he would have to go out today and that he might well be out for most of the day". Bliss told me to go for a walk, but to stay close to the stream; Storm would find me when it was safe to come back.

I left Three-Tops by the secret door and walked along the bank of the stream. Everything looked all bright and fresh. Connie had told me that this was the time of year she liked best. There were lots of lovely things to see, so many bluebells that the ground in some places looked like a blue carpet; snowdrops so white that the bright spring sunshine made them seem as though they were glowing; the yellow daffodils looked like someone had painted each one on to its stalk. If you looked closely in the grass you could see lots and lots of tiny little wild flowers getting ready for summer and the long hot days when all they had to do was bask in the sun and make the countryside look pretty. When I sat quietly on the bank of the stream, I was able to see the fish, lots and lots of them swimming in groups and the bright sunlight seemed to be dancing on the water. As I sat on the bank of the stream I knew that whatever else I wanted, I would always want to be able to walk through the countryside, run in a field, stroll through a wood and drink from a stream.

I don't know how long it was before Storm came along. "Are you alright?" he asked as he came near, "only I saw you lying so still I thought you had gone to sleep again". I told Storm what I had been thinking and he said that at least I was beginning to give some thought to my future and that was very good. Storm sat down by my side and told me that the bank of the stream was one of his favourite places and whenever he got the chance, he too loved to just sit here and enjoy what was all around him. Storm asked me not to tell any-one what he had said. "You must understand," he told me, "I have a macho image to maintain and the idea of me tip-toeing through the daffodils would do nothing at all for that image".

"Does Bliss like living in the country?" I asked him.

"Oh yes," he answered.

"How did you come to be at Three-Tops?" I asked.

"Well now," said Storm, "that's a long story. I suppose it must have all started back in history when someone decided that our breed would be ideal as guard dogs. We are big, strong, and very fast for our size and although we are very faithful and make good companions, we can manage to act and look as ferocious as a tiger with a toothache. Now take one of our famous ancestors for instance, his name was Bruno".

"That's a funny name," I said.

"Yes," said Storm, "but you must remember, this was in Germany".

"What's Germany?" I asked.

"That's the country where we originally came from". "Did I originally come from Germany?" I asked. "No silly, Labradors and even those who are nearly Labradors originated in a place called Newfoundland".

Jet, nearly a labrador

Now Bruno belonged to an aristocratic family who had a long association with the military. It was tradition in the family that all young men would first learn the discipline of the army before they were deemed ready to take their place in life. Kurt was such a young man and although there were many dogs that belonged to the family, Bruno was always to be found with Kurt. The dashing young Kurt would take Bruno with him when he and his brother officers went hunting wild boar in the forests of his beloved Germany. In the evenings Bruno would lie at the feet of his master as the young men chatted happily in the glow of the campfire. The young soldier and his dog became inseparable.

Kurt, as you would expect from a young man with his background, made rapid progress in the army and it was not long before he was in command of his own Company. Kurt's promotion meant that he was allowed to have Bruno with him all the time and the dog took to army life with all the enthusiasm of his master. But soon after Bruno joined his master, the worst possible thing happened, war broke out and it was not very long before Kurt's regiment was ordered to the front-line of the battle. The young man hated the thought of having to say goodbye to his faithful friend, but better that than risk any harm coming to Bruno by taking him to war. Bruno was sent home to the family and even though everyone tried so hard to comfort him, he was inconsolable.

The war had been going for about a year, when fate took a hand. The army asked Kurt's father if he would be willing to let them have some of his dogs to be trained as runners. Runners were dogs that would carry messages from one point of the battlefield to another. It was a very dangerous job as snipers were constantly on the lookout to prevent the runners getting to their destination and of course to intercept messages. Kurt's father had no hesitation in letting Bruno become a soldier, as he knew that his son would want the same thing for his companion. Bruno knew something of army life, so it was no surprise when he became a very good runner. He had learned the importance of discipline from being in barracks with Kurt and he also knew what it meant to obey an order to the letter.

Bruno's first posting was to an area behind his own lines and away from the battlefield, but his ability as a runner soon saw him moved up to where the battle was at its most fearsome. Bruno knew that his young master belonged to a very elite regiment and the nearer he got to the heart of the conflict, the better his chances were of meeting up with his beloved Kurt. Bruno was becoming very well known as a top dog in the ranks of the runners and it was not long before he had all the other runners on the lookout for Kurt.

One day when Bruno had been moved back for a rest, he met another runner who told him of a young company officer who just might be Kurt. The runner told Bruno where he had seen the officer. Bruno's first thoughts were to head out in search of his master, but the soldier in him would not let him do that, and besides, what would Kurt say if Bruno deserted his post and his comrades just for his own selfish reasons? No, thought Bruno, I will not shame my master and I will not leave my comrades.

The war raged on; Kurt and Bruno were constantly in each other's thoughts. Every time Kurt heard of a big battle somewhere other than his area, he would say a little prayer to the God of Runners. The war was taking a turn against Kurt's side and he and his gallant men were very soon fighting against overwhelming odds. It was not much better for Bruno and his comrades in the Corps of Runners.

All day and all night the constant shelling of each other's lines made the whole battle-front seem like a never-ending firework display, and even when there was a lull it was only to be replaced by the sound of machine-gun fire across No-Mans Land.

It was during one of the all too infrequent lulls that a wounded runner made his way to Bruno's section; he was carrying a message ordering a company commander to pull back as an attack on his position was expected and he and his men would be cut off from their own lines. Bruno, sensing that the message was destined for his master, made sure that when the call 'Company Runner' came, he was first in line to get the job of carrying the message to its destination. Bruno was all aquiver as he was shown the appropriate signs that would tell him where to take the message.

Jet, nearly a labrador

Bruno set out on his mission and it was only when he stopped to get his bearings that he became aware of a strange sensation. What was different, what was it that made him feel so strange? It was eerie and frightening, yet it was peaceful too. Bruno had the notion that maybe he had been shot by a sniper or hit by a piece of shrapnel; maybe he was dead, or at least unconscious. It was all so difficult to comprehend as he lay down and looked around him. The sun was shining and for once there were no puffs of black smoke to cut across its bright rays and, oh dear, on top of all this he had become deaf as well.

Deciding that he was neither dead nor unconscious, he continued on his way.

He was still doing his best to come to terms with what he was feeling, when he saw a gathering of troops in the distance. Are they ours or are they the enemy? He was trained to avoid any contact other than the intended recipient of whatever message he was carrying. He would skirt the troops and continue on his way, for he was quite sure in his mind where he was headed. Bruno passed as close as he dared to where the troops had camped. He heard one of them ask another if he would like a cigarette. And oh good, they were speaking in his language. Well at least the soldier offering the cigarette was, but when Bruno heard the other soldier speak, he did not sound at all the same. Poor old Bruno, what was this camp, were his other comrades prisoners or were the soldiers with the strange accents the prisoners? One thing was certain; Bruno had been trained not to take any chances as the lives of his comrades depended on him getting his message through.

The whole area was so riddled with shell holes that it was easy for Bruno to move undetected. He was some distance from the campsite when he slid into a shell hole. In the hole was a wounded soldier; the young soldier was very badly wounded in the legs and looked very, very ill. There was so much mud about that it took Bruno a little while to realise that the wounded boy was not one of his comrades. Oh dear, thought Bruno, what am I to do? I can't just leave him here to die and if I don't keep going, I will be too late to save my master and his men before they are over-run by the enemy. Bruno was feeling so guilty because he almost wished that the young man had indeed been dead. He had lost a lot of time on his mission; he knew that the attack on his master's position could start at any time. It was time to make a decision; he could not leave the wounded soldier to die in the middle of nowhere and all alone, he would have to get help from the campsite. How could he get help and be sure that he could still get his message through?

It was getting dark and that would be in his favour to avoid being shot by a sniper on the look-out for runners. The dusk would also help him to be heard, but not seen, when he made his bid to draw the troops to the wounded boy. He would have to go back to get closer to the campsite which lay beyond some hills. When Bruno reached the hills he saw a campfire, but even he knew that fires were not allowed unless you wanted to draw shellfire and sniper fire from every direction including your own. As he drew near enough to make himself heard, he braced himself and started to make enough noise to bring the whole of the two armies running. Sure enough, figures started to move towards the noise and bit by bit Bruno led them on and on until he knew they could hear the groans of the wounded soldier. He was sure that they had found the young man.

Bruno lost no time in carrying on with his mission. As he made his way in the pitch-black night, he was thinking back to the sight of the figures emerging from the campsite and it suddenly dawned on him exactly what he had seen. Yes, he had seen a number of troops, but whose troops? The more he thought about it, the more he was convinced that the troops were a mixture of both sides. Could it be, maybe the war was over, that at least would explain a lot of things; it would certainly explain why the troops at the campsite were not afraid to have a campfire. Oh dear, thought Bruno, I wish I knew for sure.

Bruno went on and just as dawn was breaking he came to a little forest on the edge of No-Mans Land. This had to be the place for which the message was intended. As Bruno crawled nearer he heard voices and yes, they were troops from his side. He listened for a little while and what he heard threw him into more confusion. If the war was over why were these troops talking about attacking an enemy

Jet, nearly a labrador

stronghold on the other side of the forest. Maybe they didn't know that the war was over. After all, as far as Bruno could tell, these troops had been the most forward of all their troops. Bruno thought it all out and decided that the war was over and at least the message would make the troops abort their plan to attack and move back towards their own lines. Bruno used all his training to approach the little band of gallant troops so as not to cause any panic.

"Hello, where have you come from?" said the sentry as Bruno got to the edge of the little camp.

"What is it, sentry?" said a voice that was like a message from heaven to the ears of a very tired and weary battle-worn runner.

The sound of Kurt's voice rejuvenated Bruno and he almost knocked his master to the ground in his excitement. "Bruno old fellow," said Kurt "what on earth are you doing out here in the middle of No-Mans Land and what is this you are carrying, a despatch pouch on your collar?". Kurt took the message from the pouch and told his sergeant to have it decoded. "Bring some food and drink for this brave runner," said Kurt. The sergeant told Kurt what the message said. From the reaction of Kurt and his men, Bruno was sure that if the war was over they hadn't heard about it, and even if the war wasn't over, his master and his little band had been isolated for so long that they no longer knew where anybody was, except for the enemy on the other side of the forest. But that's it, thought Bruno. These two little bands had become so isolated and out of reach that they had been forgotten. But what about the message that Bruno had been carrying? Well, that could have been written anytime, after all the original runner had been wounded, so who knows.

"Get ready to pull out," said Kurt, "we are going to make our way back to our lines". When they were all ready, Kurt told Bruno to lead the way and retrace his steps. Bruno was so proud to be at his master's side that he soon forgot all about his tiredness as they made their way across No-Mans Land. As they drew near to the shell hole where the young soldier had lain dying, Bruno couldn't help himself from racing ahead to see if the boy had been rescued. Kurt didn't know what to make of Bruno's behaviour as the runner went from shell hole to shell hole just to make certain that the young man was not still there. "Come on, old fellow", said Kurt, "this is no time to play around, we must get back to our lines".

As Bruno led them towards the hills where he had seen the campsite, he had to think up a plan to avoid a head-on confrontation. As they got near to the hills, Bruno once again raced on ahead. He got to the top and there it was, the campsite. What was he to do? There was only one thing for it, he would go straight into the camp and see exactly what the score was. He would have to be quick. Sure enough, the troops in the camp were from both sides. A sort of joint peace force to seek out isolated groups and inform them that the war was over.

Bruno's keen mind and his army training came into play. He saw a flag with his army's insignia on it and he knew what he must do. He snatched the pennant between his powerful jaws, and made for the

Jet, nearly a labrador

direction from which Kurt was approaching. "Halt, halt," shouted one of the soldiers. "Halt, halt," shouted another as they gave chase to Bruno.

When Bruno reached the top of the hill and he was sure that the two soldiers giving chase were wearing the right uniform, he stopped and allowed them to get near to him. As they closed in on him he dropped the pennant and as Kurt and his men came into view, what they saw was Bruno with two flag-waving comrades. It was soon clear that the war was indeed over and Kurt and his men joined the peace camp.

That evening as the men from both sides chatted to each other about things like what they wanted to do now that the terrible war was over, someone asked how the young soldier was doing who was brought in last night. Kurt asked about the young man and a fellow officer told him what had happened. How strange, thought Kurt, that Bruno must have passed near to where the wounded soldier was found and on the way here today he had acted so strangely near a certain shell hole.

The next morning Kurt asked if he could be shown the spot where the young man had been found. One of the troops who had brought the wounded boy in took Kurt to the shell hole and sure enough, it was the very same one where Bruno had acted so strangely. There was little doubt in Kurt's mind who the brave runner had been that risked so much to save the life of a wounded enemy soldier. When Kurt returned he told the officer in charge what he had discovered and that was how Bruno was decorated by both armies for bravery.

Kurt and his hero companion returned home, Kurt to go into the family business and Bruno to start a long, long line of fearless offspring to be sent all over the world.

"That is truly the best story I have ever heard in my life", I told Storm.

"I'm sure it is," said Storm, "but if we are not back at Three-Tops in time for lunch, Bliss will show us first hand what fearless really means. Come on young man, let's make tracks".

When we got back to Three-Tops, Bliss told us that she had been worried about us and she told Storm that he should know better.

Storm told Bliss that he had told me all about their famous ancestor Bruno and his master Kurt. Bliss told me to get some sleep, as we would be up very late tonight. As I tried to sleep I was thinking about the get-together and the stories.

I was all excited as I waited in the bedding store; soon they would all be coming in here and trying to decide what to do about me. I would like to stay here, but I haven't got the money to pay for my keep. I would love to work with Connie and learn all about shepherding, but I'm not sure if a Labrador should do that kind of work and besides, old Sean might not want any more helpers. It would be terrific to live at the Freshwater Restaurant but they have Annie and she is all they could possibly wish for. Bliss came into the store and told me that Annie and Connie would be here any minute; Storm had gone to wait by the secret doorway to let them in.

"Will they come together?", I asked.

"They usually do," she answered. "Well as you know, Annie has to pass by Connie's place to get here and as it is dark, it's much better and safer to walk over at the same time and they'll be company for each other".

"Oh dear," said Bliss, "we had better tidy this place up before they arrive, you know how fussy Annie is, she can't bear anything lying about where it shouldn't be and Connie will only go home and tell Sally how this place is going downhill".

"Do you think Sally will come?" I asked.

"I don't think so," said Bliss, "Sally is very old now and prefers sleeping to sitting up all night gossiping and telling stories and besides, if we asked her what we should do about you, we know exactly what she would say".

"What would she say?" I asked.

Jet, nearly a labrador

"Well, for a start,'" said Bliss, "she would tell us not to molly-coddle you and make you soft; she would no doubt go on to tell us that in her day there was no molly-coddling and if you didn't work, you didn't eat".

"Do you know," said Bliss, "one time when we had a get-together Sally got so annoyed when Polly Poodle complained about Three-Tops not having a sauna". Sally told Polly that a week looking after a flock of sheep would do her the world of good.

"A week of that my dear," said Sally "and you would be ready to settle for a dip in the stream, never mind a sauna". Polly said that the stream and chasing unruly sheep all over the countryside might suit some, but there were others who couldn't possibly do such things, what would one's friends say".

Well, Sally told Polly that the youngsters had things far too easy these days and it was small wonder that the world was in a state of chaos. "Lack of discipline," said Sally; "too much time on their hands; always thinking of themselves and never giving a thought to others".

"Oh dear, oh dear," said Bliss. I think the world of poor old Sally, but I was so relieved when Storm yawned and suggested that it was very late and we should all go to our beds. Sally was still going on about the youngsters when Connie said "Come on Sally, you know you don't mean all that, you spoiled me something terrible when I came to live with you and old Sean".

"That was different," said Sally. "You were a stranger and you were missing your family and besides I was just being hospitable".

Storm popped his head in to tell Bliss that there was no sign of Annie and Connie. Bliss told him to bring the guests along, as they would be getting impatient. I felt really important when Bliss said that I could go and wait by the secret door for Annie and Connie. It wasn't very long before they arrived and guess what, yes, old Sally had decided to come along too.

"Good evening young man," said Sally, as I showed them in. "You must be the reason for me being out of my bed instead of getting my rest".

"Now, now," said Connie, "you insisted on coming so just be nice to everyone now that you are here".

When we got into the bedding store, I was so glad to be among all my friends. "Hello Sally", said Bliss. "I'm so glad you decided to come, it wouldn't be the same without you". I had to smile because it was only that very day that I had heard Bliss telling Storm how glad she was that old Sally would not be coming tonight. This was really good, everyone was talking to everyone else and even Spick and Span joined in and they had never even met our visitors before. Tonight Sally was being particularly nice to everyone. Bliss whispered to me that Connie and Annie must have really worked on the old girl on the way here.

"I've not seen you two before," said Sally to Spick and Span. "Is this your first stay at Three-Tops?". "Yes" said Spick. "We haven't lived in this area very long". Span told Sally that their owners had returned to Yorkshire to finalise some business details and that's why he and his sister were staying at Three-Tops.

Jet, nearly a labrador

"How are you keeping?" said Lizzie Lurcher to Sally. "Oh well now my dear," replied the ageing shepherdess, "I'm enjoying my retirement, but I wake up some mornings with the odd ache here and there, but then that's just old age. Anyway, it will soon be summer and I'm looking forward to long hot days with nothing to do but lie in the sun and paddle in the cool stream".

"Well," said Connie, "you deserve a nice rest. Lord knows you've earned it".

"You are all here to see if you can help sort out young Jet's future", said Bliss, "so can we make a start?". "I think we should try to find out what the young fella wants to do," said Storm.

"So what do you want to do?" asked Bliss. "I'm not really sure," I said, "but I know that I don't want to do anything that will mean I can't be in the countryside". "Well that's a start", said Boris. "A very good start," said Alzah, "and it should help that the little chap is already in the countryside. He was very, very good when he helped me with the sheep", said Connie. "Same here." said Annie, "When I let him help to keep the birds and the rabbits off our vegetable garden, he was ever so good and if I needed help, I would be only too glad to have young Jet as an assistant."

"What about becoming a guide dog?" said Spick "If I was bigger I would like to be a guide dog". "If I was bigger I would be a police dog" said Span, "and I would arrest everyone who had ever been cruel to animals". Lizzie Lurcher said that as far as she could see, the perfect job for Jet would be gamekeeper's mate - that way he would be in the countryside, work with birds and rabbits and protect the sheep, if need be. "Very good suggestion" , said Bliss. "What do you think?" she said turning to Sally. But no one had noticed that old Sally had dozed off. "Seems like a good idea to me", said Storm, who could always be relied upon to offer only good sound advice. "What about you Jet", said Storm. "Does being a gamekeeper's mate appeal to you?". "I'm not sure," I said. "It seems like the sort of thing that a Labrador should do". "You are not all Labrador!" shouted everyone in chorus. Well, everyone except Sally, who was now fast asleep.

Boris nodded in approval when Alzah told me that I could do far worse than be a gamekeeper's mate. Lizzie Lurcher said that her mum told her that gamekeepers were kind of countryside policemen. "I know what we should do," said Bliss. "We will all keep our eyes and ears open and ask our friends to do the same. Maybe we can find a home for Jet which will allow him to do the sort of things that someone who is nearly a Labrador does".

"Well, of course, we can't always be sure of getting what we want in life," said Boris. "Sometimes we have to make the best of what we are given. Now take my great, great, great grandfather for instance. He wanted to be a famous hunter like his father and his father before him. But fate took a hand and he was given away as a present to a very aristocratic family".

"I was with a yuppie family". "Oh be quiet", said Span, "and let Boris tell us the story.". "Now, now," said Bliss. "If there is any arguing I'll make you youngsters go to bed". "That's not fair,"said Spick. "I was being really good and I was being as quiet as a mouse". "Yes, yes," said Storm, "Now I don't want to hear another word".

The family Tor was given to lived in the wilderness. They had a huge estate with woods, streams, meadows and lakes. There was game galore. Because there was so much game on the estate and the estate was so vast, it needed several gamekeepers to combat the never-ending poaching. The gamekeepers had their own dogs, and these dogs, as well as helping with the game, were trained to be ferocious as far as dealing with the poachers were concerned. There were also the wolves, so you can imagine a great deal of courage was essential if you were a gamekeeper's mate.

But there was an even bigger threat to the well-being of the families who worked and lived on the estate: bandits on horseback, who would come across the border from Mongolia to rob and kill anyone who got in their way. These bandits would also take workers and demand ransom for their return. If the employers didn't pay the ransom, the workers would be either sold on or kept as slaves.

Jet, nearly a labrador

Tor's lifestyle was very different from that of his counterparts working as gamekeeper's mates. Not for him the daily dicing with death trying to protect the estate from poachers, bandits and wolves.

Tor was given to the family as a pet and companion for Nanushka; a cheerful little girl who came to love him very dearly. The two became inseparable. Even when Nanushka was being tutored Tor was at her side. When Nanushka was not being prepared for life outside the estate, she could be found playing with the children of the estate workers and Tor was ever-present.

Although Tor came from a long line of fearless hunters who would not hesitate to tackle a wolf or indeed any wild animal single-handed, he was gentle and kind with Nanushka and her friends. The other dogs on the estate were all workers and even if they had any spare time, they would not have wanted to be seen playing with a bunch of giggling girls. Needless to say, poor old Tor was anything but popular with the gamekeepers or their mates. Sissy, parasite, loafer and even coward were just some of the insults which were levelled at him. It was a very hard life for all but the few privileged and although Nanushka's family were very kind and generous to their workers, there were those who resented their employers. Among the resentful were two brothers who worked as labourers on the estate and they were real troublemakers, but because they had wives and children, the supervisor was reluctant to sack them or even report them.

One day, when Nanushka was playing with the other children, one of the brothers told them that he had seen a very beautiful bird on one of the lakes. He told them that it had feathers for each colour in the rainbow. The children just couldn't resist the temptation to see this most unusual bird, so they arranged to sneak away one at a time so as not to be noticed.

When it was Nanushka's turn to slip away, Tor tried to stop her; he tugged and tugged at her dress, but Nanushka took no notice of him. Tor sensed that the children might be in some kind of danger, but he didn't know what.

When Nanushka and the other girls gathered near the lake, the second evil brother appeared. The evil man told the children that the rainbow bird had moved to another lake, but he would show them where it was. All the while, Tor was getting more and more worried for the safety of the children, but what could he do, they were too far away for anyone to hear, even if he did try to raise the alarm by barking as loud as he could. But Tor had no way of knowing what the danger was; all he knew was that he didn't trust the two evil brothers. Tor tried again to stop Nanushka from going any further. He tugged at her dress and even knocked her gently to the ground, but his efforts only earned him a scolding from his young mistress."

"Do behave," she told Tor, "or I will send you home and you won't see the rainbow bird".

When they had been walking for a while, the first evil brother came running up from behind them. The evil men spoke quietly to each other, but Tor knew what they were saying. One asked the other if he was certain that they were not being followed and if the children had been missed. Tor knew for certain now that his fears had not been without good cause. "Oh dear", thought Tor. "Why didn't I do something when there was only the one evil man to deal with?". Now that there were two of them, it would be more difficult if it came to a fight. One of the evil brothers told the children that it was not far to the lake and they would soon see the rainbow bird. When they came within sight of a lake, they saw some men sitting by the shores of the glistening waters.

"Oh look," said one of the children, "some other people have come to see the rainbow bird".

As they drew near to the group of men, Tor suddenly became aware of what was happening. These men by the lake were bandits from across the border and the evil brothers were delivering the children into their clutches. Tor knew that it would be futile to take the bandits on single-handed and even if went to get help, the bandits would have crossed the border with their little captives before anyone caught up with them.

Jet, nearly a labrador

Tor suddenly remembered something that might help him to save the children. Yesterday some of the gamekeepers' dogs had taunted him about how they were setting out this very morning to track down a rogue bear that had attacked a woodcutter in a wood very near the border. For once Tor was not wishing that he was off fighting killer wolves or tracking down rogue bears; he knew that his place was here with his beloved Nanushka and the other little girls. If only there was some way of getting the attention of the gamekeepers they would soon see off the bandits and rescue the children. There was only one thing for it, he would have to find a way to either keep the bandits here or at least slow them down while he tried to find the bear hunters.

When they reached the bandits, the evil brothers went up to one of them and spoke to him. That must be the leader; Tor was already working on his plan when the bandit handed one of the evil brothers something. Tor decided that it was payment for delivering the children.

By this time, even the children realised that all was not as it should be, remembering how their parents had constantly warned them of straying too far from the group of little houses where the workers lived.

"Don't cry," said Nanushka to her three little friends. "It will be all right," she assured them.

At that point, the bandit leader spoke to the girls. "That's right," he told them, "there is no need to cry, we will not harm you if you do as you are told".

Tor's mind was in turmoil and seeing the evil brothers starting back towards the workers' village, told him something that did nothing to ease his anxiety. It told Tor that the children were not going to be held for ransom, for the evil brothers were returning in the knowledge that the girls would never return to identify those who led them to the bandits. The children were to be sold and would never see their families again.

Four bandits armed to the teeth. What was Tor to do? One thing became very clear in his mind; the Bandits would not want him around for very much longer; they would sell him off to a poacher or even worse. It was now or never. Tor had only one thing on his side: the element of surprise. After all, up to now he had looked nothing more than a pet to be played with by four little girls, so he was no threat to the bandits. That must have been exactly how the bandit

leader saw Tor, for he hardly gave him a second glance. It was when the bandit leader told his henchmen it was time to go that Tor went into action. He moved so fast that all the bandit leader knew about the movement was the terrible pain that shot through his evil body as Tor drove his fangs into the calf of his leg. The confusion that reigned allowed Tor to do the same to the bandit who had gone to fetch their horses.

With terror in the hearts of the bandits and bedlam all around, it was time for the next part of Tor's plan. He made for the four horses that had been loosely tied to a tree. There was no time to be half-hearted;

Jet, nearly a labrador

if he was to be sure of scattering the horses beyond recall, he would have to fill them with terror. He took an almighty leap and landed on the back of one of the horses. He clawed his way up its neck and sunk his teeth into one of its ears. The animal shrieked with pain and before the bandits could do anything to stop their panic-stricken steeds, they were off and soon disappearing into the distance.

There was one last thing to do before Tor set off in search of the gamekeepers. He made his way back to where Nanushka and her little friends were huddled together. There was noise and pandemonium all about him as he snatched the little rag doll that Nanushka carried everywhere with her.

Not knowing anything of Tor's plan, Nanushka was as bewildered as the bandit leader had been when her hero first went into action and with tears flowing down her cheeks, she watched as he deserted her, taking her doll with him. The pain of leaving his beloved Nanushka and her little friends tugged at his heartstrings and Tor made his one and only error of judgment; he half-turned to try and assure his beloved companion that he would be back. Tor felt the searing pain in his side before he heard the crack of the rifle. Despite the pain, he knew that all that stood between a life of slavery for the children or their rescue was the courage handed down to him by his forefathers, any one of whom would have done what he had to do now.

The rag doll between his powerful jaws and the knowledge that the doll would help him to alert the gamekeepers, helped Tor to put the pain to the back of his mind. The one consolation was that if he was wounded, there were four bandits trying to abduct four children while on foot and two of the bandits were in just as much pain as him. Tor had a good idea of where the gamekeepers might be and as he sensed that he was going in the right direction, he drew on all his inherited strength, speed and hunting instincts. Soon he was sure that he could hear the baying of the other dogs as they tracked down the rogue bear. The noise from the hunters increased and Tor knew that they had cornered their prey. He would have to drive himself even harder before the hunters had done what they had set out to do before moving off. The hunters were far too occupied with their conquest to notice the brave Tor coming ever closer, the wound in his side bleeding profusely and sapping his strength every bit as much as the physical effort. He was almost up to them when his poor body gave way to sheer exhaustion.

"Look there," said one of the men. "Is that who I think it is?"

"Yes," said another. "It's Nanushka's pet waster. What on earth is he doing out here?"

Tor had collapsed on to the wounded side of his body. The men couldn't see the wound and they made fun of Tor, saying that he must have gone for a stroll and got lost and then passed out with fear. Tor lay motionless and it was only when one of their hunting dogs found the rag doll that the men became alarmed, for the doll had blood on it. One man knelt down and examined Tor and the wound was discovered. But where was Nanushka? everyone knew that the little girl and her dog were inseparable. And the blood on the rag doll – was that Tor's blood or had something terrible happened to the little one? The headman told one of the others to ride back as fast as his horse could carry him and bring the master and all the help he could find.

"See to him," he told another, "stay with him and the rest of us will follow his tracks back to wherever he came from."

It was easy for the hunting dogs to follow Tor's trail. On the way they found a loose horse, then another, and as the animals were tacked up for riding, the men just didn't know what to make of it all. When they reached the lake the men, being gamekeepers, looked around for signs that might help them to figure out some of what they had seen. The spot where the horses had been tied told them that something or someone had frightened the horses. Nearby, some empty cartridge shells were proof that Tor had probably been shot there. There were signs of many people having been there and closer inspection told the expert huntsmen that the people had met there by coming from opposite directions. The horsemen had come from the direction of the border and the other party with the unmistakable footprints of children had come from the direction of their very own village. But what had

Jet, nearly a labrador

the children been doing so far from the village. And who did the adult footprints belong to that had brought them there? Surely no-one from the village would be silly enough to venture so close to the border without a proper escort? The terrible truth was emerging with each new piece of the puzzle. So it became clear, the men all agreed, that a small group of children had been coaxed or led to the shores of the lake and had either been taken by force or simply handed over to some people from across the border. There was no time to figure out or try to find a reason for the stray horses. The chances were that as the trail showed no signs of horse tracks going in the direction of the border, the children and their captors were still on this side.

The men and their hunting dogs set off in pursuit. There was not a minute to spare. The men would have to rely on the dogs to follow the trail at great speed. There could be no room for error and nor could the dogs allow themselves to be fooled by false trails. The dogs were highly trained and knew when to follow a trail in silence so as not to alert the prey. The gait of the lead dog told his master that they were closing in on their prey.

"Halt!" said the headman. "We must make a plan."

The men knew that it was only a matter of time before their master and reinforcements joined them.

"This is what we will do," said the headman, "two of us will stay on the trail and the rest of you will make a sweep and put yourselves between them and the escape route to the border. We will then close in on them and try to rescue the children."

It was very shortly after that the master arrived with some more helpers. The master told how the village was devastated at the loss of the children. The head gamekeeper told the master all about what they had found at the lake, but who had led the children to the lake? Everyone on the estate had been accounted for. It was clear now that whoever it was, did indeed hand the children over at the lake and then returned to the village.

"Don't worry," said the master, "When we rescue the children we will find out who it was that could be guilty of such an abominable act. Was Tor alright?"

"Yes," answered the gamekeeper. "His wound has been looked after and when he is rested he can be moved."

The gamekeeper said that the men he had sent ahead to the border would be in position now and whoever had the girls would be in the middle.

"We can move in on them now."

The hunters began to move a lot quicker and before very long they had sight of the bandits and the children. The master fired a shot from his rifle. The men who were coming at the bandits from the opposite direction answered the shot. The bandits, realising that their position was hopeless, gave themselves up.

The children came running to the hunters and all they wanted to know was if Tor was all right. The children were all talking about how Tor had bitten two of the bandits and then scared their horses into running away. Nanushka told her father how the evil brothers had lured them to the lake with the story of a rainbow bird.

When they got back to the village there was great rejoicing, Nanushka's mother said that everyone should come to the manor that evening where there would be a grand party with music and dancing and lots to eat and drink.

Although the evil brothers ended up in jail, Nanushka's kind parents allowed their wives and children to live on in their little houses.

Tor was soon up and about and never again was he to be the object of fun; the hunting men and their dogs respected him and they paid him the best compliment they could when they asked if Tor would lead all the hunting dogs in the annual wild boar hunt, an honour only bestowed on the very bravest hunters in all the land. Nanushka agreed, but she told Tor that he could lead the hunt just this one time as she still hadn't quite forgiven him for snatching her rag doll from her.

Jet, nearly a labrador

"That's the best story I have ever heard in my whole life," I told Boris.

"It was a lovely story," said Bliss "But it does not help to get you sorted out, young man. It's very, very late now so we will have to have another get-together and have another try at working out what to do with you. In the meantime you may continue to stay here at Three-Tops with us. At least that way we will be able to keep an eye on you."

"Come Sally," said Connie as she gently woke her aged friend "Time to go home".

"Oh dear," said Sally, "You must excuse me - I must have closed my eyes for a minute or two."

As it was very, very late, Storm offered to walk the girls home.

Annie said, "Thank you Storm, but I must run all the way home so that I am there when the last customers leave the restaurant."

Connie was glad to accept Storm's offer, as she had to walk slowly with old Sally. Bliss said that we would all meet again on Sunday night.

Before Connie left, she said that as Saturday was a very busy day at Annie's, I could spend the day with her and help with the sheep.

"Would you like that?" Bliss asked me.

"Yes please," I said.

"Come then," said Bliss. "You had better get some sleep. Goodnight Annie, goodnight Jet, goodnight Connie".

"Goodnight Jet, goodnight Lizzie"

"Goodnight Jet, goodnight Boris."

"Goodnight Jet, goodnight Alzah."

"Goodnight Jet, goodnight Spick and Span."

"Goodnight Jet, goodnight Sally."

"Go to sleep young man, it's way past your bedtime. Honestly, the youngsters today; thoroughly spoiled, thoroughly spoiled."

"Yes," said Bliss, "You're quite right Sally."

"Will we see you on Sunday evening?" Bliss asked.

"Not likely," said Sally. "Once in a blue moon is quite enough for me to be out gallivanting at this time of night, young lady."

I spent Saturday and Sunday helping Connie with her sheep. I told Connie that I could hardly wait for Sunday evening to come.

"Someone might tell us another great story."

"They might," said Connie, "But that's not the reason for the get-together."

At last it was Sunday evening and as we waited in the bedding store for Annie and Connie to arrive, we talked amongst ourselves. Bliss told Spick and Span that she overheard the manager's wife telling him about a phone call she had received.

"It was from your owners," she told them. "They will be coming for you on Tuesday morning."

"Oh crikey!" said Span, "Just as I was getting to like it here! it's always the same."

"It's our master's job you know," said Spick, "He's what they call a trouble-shooter."

"Does he really shoot people who make trouble?" I asked.

"Silly boy," said Storm. "It means that he is very good at solving problems."

"Oh good," said Lizzy Lurcher; "Maybe we can get him to solve the problem of Jet and how to find him a nice owner who likes the idea of tramping around the countryside all day long."

"Not *all* day long?" I said innocently.

Jet, nearly a labrador

"There, there" said Bliss, "It's alright Jet, Lizzie was just being a little tetchy. It's not that she is sarcastic by nature, she is very kind and loving, but every so often she gets a bit frustrated at not being able to do what she was born to do."

"What was she born to do?" I asked.

"Well," said Boris, "Why don't we let Lizzie tell us herself."

By this time, Annie and Connie had arrived.

"In a perfect world for dogs," said Lizzie, "I would be owned by a family of travellers, or a poor family with lots of little mouths to feed or even some hermit who lived off the land. I would be the only thing that made the difference between someone having enough to eat or starvation; I would be the huntress I was born to be. And most of all, I would retain my dignity in the knowledge that I was earning my keep. It's not that my master is not a kind man, and heaven knows, my mistress could not be nicer if she was my own mum, but there is so much they just don't understand about me. For instance, once when they took me to visit some friends I finished up in real trouble through no fault of my own.

"What happened was their friend gave me loads of dinner; I lay down on the lawn and fell asleep in the hot sun. I must have been dreaming about the old days when dogs were allowed to do what comes naturally. I remember opening my eyes and thinking what a lovely life it was, nothing to do and all day to do it, all the food and pampering that a body could want and a doting pair of owners to answer to my every whim. What more could a dog wish for? I was about to find out, so were my owners. If only they would understand.

"As I emerged from the land of nod, I heard the sweet song of a blackbird. I lay very still for fear of frightening the singer. I was lost in the beauty of Mrs. Blackbird's melody when out of the corner of my eye I saw it, the crouched figure of the hunter stealthily moving in the direction of my serenader. The scene of the hunter and the prey, which has been part of nature since time began, was all too much for my domestic side to cope with. Nature took over and another hunter entered the arena as I prepared to join in. As the feline assassin licked its lips in anticipation of Sunday lunch, I only wanted to have some fun. I had no intention of harming the moggy, but I was going to enjoy the next few seconds.

As the cat stalked his prey, little did he know that he too was no more than a prey for an equally skilful hunter. Does a leopard change its spots? I asked myself as I remained motionless; you are what you are and no amount of domesticity can wipe out completely everything that is second nature to you. Mrs Blackbird continued to sing; the moggy moved ever closer and my whole body became a coiled spring. If poor old Mrs Blackbird was to give a repeat performance tomorrow then I was going to have to get my timing right. The muscles of the moggy tightened and that was my signal to go into action. My shout of 'Super-Liz' was enough to send Mrs Blackbird home to her kids as the moggy and yours truly collided in mid-air, about halfway between the ground and the spot on top of the fence from which the winged warbler had given her version of 'In a Monastery Garden.'

"Pick on someone your own size," I told the feline fiend as he landed on the ground.

"You mind your own business," he shouted at me as he poked out his paw and scratched me on the nose.

Jet, nearly a labrador

I know I said that I didn't mean the moggy any harm, but as I chased him round and round the gardens, marmalised moggy was uppermost in my mind. The begonias were battered, the roses were ruined, the trailing lobelia was thrashed, a mother-in-laws tongue was massacred and this busy lizzie was bashed with a brush and put into the car in disgrace until it was time to go home."

"Not exactly the gardener's favourite flower then?" suggested Bliss.

"Certainly not," said Lizzie. "Come to think of it, we have never been invited back to that house".

"Now then," said Storm "What are we going to do about our little friend Jet?"

Bliss said that they were not pushing me out, but it was best for me if I could find a permanent home sooner rather than later. "However", said Storm "if it's still alright for the young fella to spend some time at Annie's and Connie's then we will carry on the way we are".

Annie said that it was alright with her. Connie said the same and anyway, she was almost sure that old Sean knew all about Jet helping with the sheep as all of a sudden the food rations had almost doubled.

"Now that's a coincidence," said Annie. "I've noticed that at Freshwater too. Do you suppose my master knows about Jet?"

"I wouldn't be at all surprised," said Bliss. "After all, if old Sean does know, then it would be fair to assume that your owners know. In fact, if old Sean knows then everybody for miles around will know; you know what he's like when he has a few drinks on Saturday night in the Freshwater Restaurant."

"How strange," said Bliss, "Storm and I were just saying only this afternoon how our meals had suddenly increased in size."

"Could it be," said Storm "that all our owners know about Jet and they are willing to turn a blind eye."

"Seems likely," said Boris "and why not as Jet is a great help for all of you."

"Well maybe they do know and maybe they don't, but all the same I think we should be careful, at least for a little while longer. We don't want him sent back to that family where he was so unhappy" said Bliss.

"And we don't want to see him put in jail for being a vagrant," said Spick.

"What's a vagrant?" asked Span.

"Someone who has no place to stay and wanders the streets," answered Spick.

Alzah, who was not one for saying very much at any time, decided that he would have something to say on the subject of my future.

"I don't think being a vagrant is all that bad," said Alzah, "You can go to different places and see all the things that some others only hear about and you can make lots and lots of new friends. After a while you would have friends everywhere and no matter where you found yourself you would never be lonely. Look at Jet, he has made more new friends in a short time than some others make in a year or more and he is having a wonderful time, much, much better than when he had a fixed address. Look at all the new things he has learned about shepherding, patrolling, vegetable protection and best of all, he is learning to be a survivor which is very, very important, especially when you are only 'nearly a Labrador'."

Jet, nearly a labrador

"I am a Labrador," I said.

"No you're not," said Boris. "Now be quiet and pay attention to your elders."

"He looks like a Labrador to me," said Span "and you lot shouldn't pick on him just because he's a vagabond."

They all laughed as Bliss told Span that I was a vagrant and not a vagabond.

Spick apologised for Span, saying that her brother was always embarrassing her by getting things mixed up.

"Once" said Spick, "when we were staying with some friends, one of them was boasting about how clever her master was and how he was so good at all sports. Span said that our master was also very clever and he had a black belt in origami." Alzah said that one of his ancestors had been a vagrant and he did all right for himself

"What was his name" asked Spick.

"Well," said Alzah, "his name was Aliba, at least that was the name given to him by the leader of the bandits who stole him when he was only a youngster."

"What was his name before he was stolen?" asked Boris.

"Baba was his name, so when the bandits stole him they took a BA away and added an ALI. If they had just added the ALI we would have had the same name as the most notorious thief in history."

"Who was that?" asked Span.

"Ali-Baba," said Alzah.

"Was he really famous?" asked Lizzie.

"Oh yes," said Alzah, "he was just as famous as your Robin Hood and he had books written about him and a film about him and his gang. It was called 'Ali-Baba and his Forty Thieves'."

"Who did the bandits steal Aliba from?" asked Spick.

"A son of a King" said Alzah. "In those days when a Prince became of age, he would set up his own principality, a kind of kingdom within a kingdom. Only the Prince and his followers would live in the mountains far away from his parents and their palace."

"Did the King and the Queen make the Prince leave home?" Lizzie asked.

"Not really," Alzah told her. "The Prince was expected to go out into the world to learn all about living amongst the people and earn their respect. After all, the Prince would one day be expected to take over from his father, the King".

"Was Aliba very unhappy when he was stolen by the bandits?" asked Span.

"At first he was," said Alzah, "but he soon grew very fond of the bandit leader's daughter; she was called Almirah".

"Was Almirah very beautiful?" asked Spick.

"Oh yes," said Alzah. He told us that once upon a time Almirah had been a Princess back in her own little country, but her wicked uncle turned their army against her father and they were lucky to escape with their lives. Almirah had not seen her mother for years and didn't even know if she was alive. The wicked uncle had either banished all the good people or locked them up in the castle dungeons.

"When did Almirah's father become a bandit?" asked Lizzie.

"Well," said Alzah, "when the King was forced out of his country, he took with him lots and lots of poor families to save them from being turned into slaves by his wicked brother, but everywhere they went they were moved on. Eventually they settled in the wilderness on a stretch of land that was not owned by any one country in particular, although many laid claim to it.

The exiled King and his people found safety on the land that nobody

Jet, nearly a labrador

else dared claim for themselves for fear of starting a war. Although the King and his people got some help from the many small countries that surrounded them, it was not enough to sustain them, so the King was forced into becoming a bandit.

"Was Almirah a bandit?" asked Spick.

"Not at first," said Alzah, "but it was not long before she was riding by her father's side when they raided the far off rich kingdoms and soon people were talking about the beautiful bandit Princess who stole to feed her people".

Aliba too was becoming famous, for he was ever by the side of his mistress. More and more poor people came from far and near to join the exiled King and the bandit Princess and before long it was as though a new little country was growing in the very place that only a short time before had been just a wasteland; a place so barren and godforsaken, that travellers went round it rather than across it. Word went from village to village, from town to town and from country to country, that there was a place where people could be free from tyranny, a place where everyone shared everything and all men were treated as equals.

Soon the great camel trains were calling; the people of the new settlement could trade the things they made for other things and the exiled King and his Princess all but gave up being bandits.

Whenever they heard about rulers being cruel or unfair to their people, the bandit King and Princess would lead their band of faithful followers in raids against the tyrants. Money, jewels and livestock would be taken in the dead-of-night; prisoners and slaves would be freed and taken back to a life of freedom in the new settlement. As time went by, rulers of other places came to visit the new settlement to learn something of the peace that reigned there. Among the rulers that came to visit was a young Prince who had been sent out into the world by his parents to learn about life with ordinary people.

The young Prince was overwhelmed by Almirah's beauty and very soon he was a regular visitor to the settlement. Nobody paid much attention to the fact that Aliba and the young Prince became more and more good friends with each visit. Normally Aliba would not leave Almirah's side for anyone else. One morning, Almirah was devastated to find that Aliba was missing. Where could he be, what could have happened to him? Almirah was heartbroken at the thought of not seeing her beloved loyal friend ever again. Almirah's father gathered his best men and their fastest horses and told them to go out in all directions in search of Aliba. It was almost night-time when a man rode into the settlement and told Almirah that Aliba was safe and sound in a small principality to the north of the settlement. There was no time to waste on wondering what Aliba was doing in this other place or how he came to be there. When they reached the principality, Almirah was taken to the ruler who was none other than the young Prince. The young man had been injured and was in bed. Almirah didn't know what to say or do; should she inquire after Aliba or ask the Prince what happened to him and if he was all right? The Princess was saved the trouble when the young man told her to sit down and he would tell her all she wanted to know.

The Prince told Almirah how he was on his way home from her settlement when his horse was frightened and threw him. The horse ran home leaving him lying injured and at the mercy of the wild animals that roamed the wastelands. He tried to crawl, but the pain from his broken leg was so great that he decided to wait to be rescued. He knew that his horse would return for him before very long. He was being stalked by a pack of hungry wolves and feared the worst. He was slipping in and out of consciousness because of the terrible pain from his leg, which had been shattered by the fall from his horse. He was sure it was the end when he heard what he thought to be the sound of the wolves fighting amongst themselves to decide whom he belonged to. There was only one thing for it; he would just have to do his best to stay alive until help arrived.

He drew his sword and dragged himself towards the squabbling wolves. He lashed out and struck into the pack. The wolves began to disperse and it was only then that he realised he was not alone in his fight for life. The sight of Aliba's powerful frame surrounded by four

Jet, nearly a labrador

snarling wolves spurred him on. The shattered leg no longer gave off the terrible pains of earlier; his head was clear and his arm strong as he lunged to the aid of the gallant canine warrior. In that moment, the young Prince was sure that the hound who had so readily befriended him that first time they met at the settlement was indeed Baba, the pet who had been stolen from him.

When the Prince had finished telling Almirah all about how he and Aliba had been rescued, she told him that his pet Baba had not really been stolen; Baba had tried to protect the King's property and had even chased Almirah and her father across the wilderness until he could go no further. They couldn't just leave him at the mercy of the wolves, so they took him to the settlement. News was sent to the young man's parents and very soon they visited their son.

The Prince told his father all about what had happened in Almirah's country and how her father was forced into becoming a bandit. The King told Almirah's father that if he would swear to give up being a bandit he would march his army on the wicked brother and overthrow him.

Soon Almirah's father was once again King in his own country and reunited with his captive wife. The wicked brother was banished; Almirah and her young Prince were married and became the King and Queen of a very very happy and peaceful little kingdom called "Aliba".

"That's the best story I have ever heard in my whole life," I told Alzah.

Lizzie Lurcher was crying and said that she loved stories that had happy endings.

Boris asked Alzah if Aliba was badly hurt when he fought the wolves.

"Well," said Alzah, "Aliba was quite badly wounded, but he soon recovered and went on to have lots and lots of offspring".

"Come now," said Bliss, "it's time to go to bed".

Annie and Connie, who had been so quiet all evening, were now asking Alzah all kinds of questions:

"Did Almirah have lots of children? where was the wicked brother banished to? did the little kingdom grow and grow and grow into a big country? was Aliba your great-great-great-great-grandfather?"

Question after question was hurled at poor old Alzah until Boris came to the rescue saying that if Annie and Connie did not hurry up, he would not walk them home.

I went to bed thinking about how brave Aliba had been to fight all those wolves and I couldn't help thinking over and over in my mind, how did Aliba know that the young Prince was lying somewhere with a broken leg and about to be set upon by a pack of hungry wolves? Still, it was a great story and I was sure that every word of it was true.

The next morning I set out for the Freshwater Restaurant. I called on Connie on the way; she told me that there was a search going on all over the countryside for a very dangerous criminal who was part of a gang of robbers. Connie said as the police were searching all along the banks of the stream, it might be safer for me to take a different route to Freshwater.

I wasn't sure of the way overland, so I decided to take the main road which I knew went past Annie's. I was almost at Freshwater when it all happened. All of a sudden there were police everywhere; wailing sirens; blue flashing lights; men rushing about in all directions and police dogs barking. It was obvious that the criminal had been uncovered and the police were about to capture him.

Without a thought, I jumped over a wall and finished up in someone's garden, where some chickens immediately began to squawk and run about flapping their wings as though they were about to be murdered. I tried to calm them down, but it was no good, – the poor old things were panic-stricken and the more I tried, the louder they squawked until there was nothing else for it, but to get out of the garden as fast as I could. I was about to understand what Old Sally had told me about things not always being what they seemed. The sound of the

Jet, nearly a labrador

chickens trying to outdo the wailing of the police sirens and the sight of yours truly coming over the garden wall was quite all the evidence that one fresh faced police constable required to make an arrest and before you could say 'Fresh Farm Eggs', I was on my way to where you find me now: the local nick for vagrants, vagabonds, runaways and out-and-out villains. Whatever would my old mum say if she knew that one of her offspring had finished up in jail? A common criminal, an outcast from society, a social leper and all because I was given as a present to a family who just didn't know the first thing about my needs, apart from feeding me and quenching my thirst. What next, I ask myself, what next indeed.

Annie is going to be really worried by now. I should have been at Freshwater hours ago and goodness knows what everyone at Three-Tops will think when I don't show up there. If only there was some way I could let all my friends know where I am, at least that would save them from thinking all kinds of things. I wouldn't want Storm and Bliss thinking that I had just up and left without even bothering to say goodbye, especially since they had been so kind to me. Oh dear, suppose I'm taken back to that terrible house I ran away from, what then?

I was only going to hide in that garden and never had any intention of hurting those chickens. If only that criminal had not come into my area, if only I had not jumped over that garden wall, if only Connie had not suggested taking a different route to Freshwater, if only this and if only that! Look on the bright side, I might be adopted by a family of aristocrats or even a Prince or Princess, just like in the stories at Three-Tops, or I might turn out to be a famous hero like Tor or Bruno or Aliba.

"What's this one's name?" asks an old lady, peering through the bars at me. "Has he got an owner, has he been lost, is he in need of a home?"

"We don't really know anything about him," the kennel gaoler tells her. "He is waiting to be assessed and we must check to find out if he has been reported missing by anyone".

"He's certainly full of life," says the old lady, "A bit too boisterous for me, I'm afraid".

Hello, there's that policeman who arrested me. I wonder what he's doing here? He's coming this way, now the head gaoler is talking to him. The policeman tells the gaoler that he can't find any missing report for me; he also tells him that none of the chickens came to any harm.

"Oh," he says, "there's no doubt that the poor old chickens had one heck of a fright, but from what I could see of it, it was a toss-up who was the most frightened, our canine friend or the feathered egg layers".

Very funny Mr Policeman, that will do my image a lot of good around here. Not that I see myself as being macho mind you, because us Labradors are more your sensitive, intellectual types, you understand. All the same, you can't be too careful in a place like this.

Hello, Shamus the nutty Red Setter is at it again. Can't be quiet for more than a couple of minutes at a time, that one. Any minute now Spike the Staffordshire Bull will tell him to be quiet. Buster the Boxer will tell Spike to lay off Shamus and pick on someone in his own league. Jockie the Scottie will tell Spike not to butt in to other folks

Jet, nearly a labrador

business and Penelope Pointer will tell everyone to be quiet as she can feel one of her migraines coming on. Of course, all this small-time bickering is beneath someone like me who has been around a bit, so I'll just let them get on with it.

Three days in nick and I am bored to tears, I wish I was back with my friends at Three-Tops. I do miss them all. I can just see Bliss doing her 'I'm in charge bit' and telling the others to be sensible and not to worry as I (Jet) am probably curled up on someone's rug while being waited on hand and foot. Storm will be saying that I can look after myself because of what he taught me. Alzah and Boris will nod in agreement, while Lizzie Lurcher will be saying how she wished she'd been able to teach me a thing or two about life. Spick and Span will be united with their owners and settling into the new homestead. Connie Collie will have one eye on her flock and one eye on the surrounding countryside just in case yours truly is wandering around suffering from amnesia or just plain stupidity by getting myself lost. I'll bet Annie Alsatian is wishing that I was with her and helping to keep the birds and rabbits off her vegetable garden.

I wonder if I will ever see them all again. But I must not get downhearted. As old Sally would say, where there's life, there's hope and she should know, for she must be a hundred years old if she's a day and she never gets down in the dumps. I wonder where I'll be and what I'll be doing when I reach a hundred, that is of course if I don't die from malnutrition in this place first. I couldn't half do with one of Annie's midday snacks this minute; a nice piece of roast pork or a leg of chicken or even a bit of scrag-end, all crispy and dunked in nice brown gravy followed by a bowl of milky rice pudding. I'd better stop this hallucinating over food or I'll finish up in a funny farm herding fairies or looking for dolls in a cabbage patch!

Hello, here comes one of the gaolers. What's that she's got, a lead? No way Fanny, I am not being harnessed like a donkey. Get off you silly girl, how would you like to be half-strangled every time you went for a walk? OK then, no need to send for the heavy mob, I'll come quietly. Nice countryside and look, there's a river. I have a feeling that I have been here before. If only I could get free from this lead I could investigate. I'm sure I've been along this way before. What's that noise I can hear in the distance? Sounds like a flock of sheep fussing about. One thing is sure; I am not going to be let off this lead so I'll just have to pull Miss Piggy towards the bleating. I knew it; I just knew it, that's Connie Collie's flock of sheep.

It's all coming back to me now and I am getting my bearings. Oh, if only I was off this lead. So near and yet so far! In one direction lies Freshwater and my friend Annie Alsatian and in the opposite direction lies Three-Tops and Storm and Blizzard and all my other friends and here am I being led around on a lead with no chance of seeing any of them.

One slip, Miss Piggy, just one slip, one split second of dopiness and I shall be off before you can say 'Jack Flash'. I wonder, I just wonder, no, she will never fall for that one, the 'thorn-in-the foot'. Why not and anyway, what have I got to lose? Right then, here goes.

"Ouch, ouch, oh the pain, oh dear, I can't bear it, oh the pain is excruciating, my foot's dropping off!".

Jet, nearly a labrador

Come on then, dopey, have a look, good girl. Now let go of the lead so that you can use both hands. That's it, put the lead on the ground, good girl. Now tell me to lie down; that way the choke chain will go slack around my neck. Oh you are a little darling, a bit dopey, but a little darling all the same. Freedom at last, but I do hope poor old Miss Piggy doesn't get into trouble over my escape. I'll make for Three-Tops. Storm and Bliss will take me in and they can call a get-together with Annie Alsatian and Connie Collie and help me to decide what I should do next.

When I reached Three-Tops, I walked around the perimeter fence knowing that sooner or later I would meet Storm doing his rounds. I could have gone in by way of the secret entry, but I thought it best to wait to be invited in. It wasn't very long before Storm appeared and true to form, his first words were, "Where in the hell have you been, you stupid boy, you've had us out of our minds with worry?"

I started to explain, but Storm said that explanations could wait. We made our way to the bedding store and it was only when I was actually inside that I felt safe and secure. I hardly had time to get my breath back before Bliss appeared doing her mother-hen impersonation.

"You naughty, naughty boy," she scolded as she walked up and down the store. "What on earth have you been up to and where in heaven's name have you been? Have you had anything to eat, are you hurt anywhere, are you ill? Oh you silly, silly boy".

After Bliss had finished and Storm had told all the guests that yours truly was back. I told them what had happened and how I finished up in the nick. When I told them how I escaped, Storm laughed and said that I must have learned something from all those stories told to me by all my friends.

Bliss scolded Storm and told him not to encourage me as she was sure that I could be daft enough without any help from him. Bliss said that I was not to go outside Three-Tops until there had been a get-together to see what was to become of me.

That evening I was allowed to stay up late and join in the chatting with Bliss, Storm and the guests.

"What was it like inside?" asked Basher Bates the Bull Terrier. "Did they duff you up? they duffed me up when I was inside".

I knew Basher from when I lived with the Yuppie family so I asked him if they had been looking for me.

"Not likely," said Basher "In fact, you did old Fancy-Pants a favour when you scarpered. She told my mistress that you were becoming a handful. Mind you, she had her work cut out with that demonic brat of hers. No disrespect you understand, but two head-bangers under the one roof can be a bit trying for anyone".

Saucy monkey, I thought as I glared at Basher. Mind you, I made sure he was not looking in my direction as I glared.

"What was the grub like?" asked Dinky Dachshund "I'll bet the screws stood over you to make sure you ate it".

I told Dinky that the food wasn't too bad, but there was just not enough of it.

"Now, now," said Bliss, "enough talk of things not very nice, let's talk of nice things".

Bliss said that Storm would make arrangements for a get-together with Annie and Connie within the next few days. "In the meantime" said Bliss "we must all help to make Jet feel welcome at Three-Tops".

I felt really happy when I heard Bliss say that and as I looked round me I thought how lucky I was to have such good friends, but I was also a little sad because I was the only one who didn't have a home of my own. It seemed strange that I should be mixing with the well-offs when I had nothing and not many prospects either. The guests at Three-Tops had all belonged to people who didn't have to worry about where the next meal was coming from to say the least, and as you can imagine, their pets had a cushy old life. I desperately wanted a fixed abode. I didn't want to be a pampered pooch, but neither did I long for a life of deprivation. I had seen the results of abject poverty in the shape of little Minnie. Little Minnie was a crossbreed (what you humans call a mongrel), which I saw in the nick. Minnie, like yours

Jet, nearly a labrador

truly, was a Christmas present to a family, but unlike mine, Minnie's family had more than the one child.

The story goes that Minnie and the children got on very well and played together for hours and hours each day. To cut a long story short and to skirt around some of the more heart-rending details, Minnie's master lost his job and from then on things got progressively worse for the unfortunate family.

The family were split up and Minnie was farmed out to a relative. Minnie missed the children so much that at every opportunity she left her new home in search of them. On more than one occasion, poor little Minnie was found exhausted and very much the worse for wear and returned to her new home.

It was on one of her searches that poor Minnie fell prey to the amorous advances of a street urchin. Minnie became pregnant and her new owner disowned the poor luckless wretch. She was taken into care and when she whelped, her four little ones were placed in good homes just as soon as they were weaned. Minnie was sad that she had not had more time with her offspring, but she was relieved that they had been at least found good homes. The good bit about the tale of Minnie is that it had a happy ending. I had heard in the nick that there was a very nice elderly couple who had been looking for a small pet and they had been quite taken with little Minnie. They would be taking her to live with them in their nice little country cottage.

When I had told the story of little Minnie to my friends at Three-Tops, they were sad and happy, sad for the family, but happy that little Minnie would be well looked after and able to give lots of love in return.

Bliss told the others that they should never miss a chance to show their love to their owners, especially when their owners were being kind and considerate.

Storm said that was all very good, but what do you do when an owner is being horrible and beastly? There will always be some owners who will be less than kind from time to time, but by-and-large the majority are alright and it's the pet who learns to handle them that gets the best out of them, said Bliss.

"Did your owner beat you - is that why you left home in the first place?" asked Daisy Dalmatian.

I had not met Daisy before, so I had to explain everything to her. Daisy was very understanding, and said that if ever I was in her neck of the woods, I should call on her.

Daisy's owners were very rich; they lived in a mansion with acres and acres of land on all sides.

"Why don't you tell us all about your life at Havalot House?" Bliss asked of Daisy.

"Oh I couldn't," said Daisy coyly.

"Oh please do," said Basher Bates. "I'm just dying to hear about a bunch of ponces living off the fat of the land while poor old geezers like my guv'nor have to slave from dawn to dusk just to keep their barnet above water".

"Now, now, Basher Bates, you speak for yourself," said Polly Poodle, who lived only a couple of doors from Basher. "We want to hear all about life at Havalot House".

"You would," said Basher "And no wonder. Do you know" he said addressing the rest of us, "her mistress spends her life trying to climb the social ladder and she still hasn't managed to get further up than the first rung".

"Oh you beast," cried Polly. "At least my mistress does not swindle people left, right and centre like some we know".

"That'll do," said Storm. "That's quite enough bickering for now. Go on Daisy, tell us about life at Havalot."

"Well," said Daisy, "I am not just a pet as some people might think. I have a job to do like everyone at Havalot. There are all kinds of dogs and horses on the estate and there are cattle and sheep and game birds

Jet, nearly a labrador

of every description and there are all sorts of pests and vermin and all these have to be managed in very different ways. For instance, Tish, Tosh and Tiny are terriers that help the gamekeepers to control the vermin. Then there's Flick and Flack the sheep dogs who help the herdsmen with the cattle and the sheep. Then there's Bow and Arrow, the two greyhounds who are so fast they can outrun any wild animal. Then there's Seek and Find, a Labrador and a Retriever who work with the men who manage the game birds.

"That's what I would like to do," I told Daisy.

"Oh be quiet," said Basher, "you're only nearly a Labrador".

"My mum was a Labrador," I told the bossy Bull Terrier.

"What is your job at Havalot?" asked Polly Poodle. "I'll bet you have the best job of all".

"Well now," said Daisy, "I must admit I would not be telling the truth if I did not say that my life at Havalot is very pleasant indeed. Most of the time I am a companion to her ladyship and the rest of my time is spent working as a coach dog".

"What's a coach dog?" asked Polly.

"Well," said Daisy, "in the old days a long, long time ago, Dalmatians would accompany their owners almost everywhere they went. They would run behind their coach, placing themselves dead centre between the rear wheels and close to the axle. They would not allow anything or anybody to distract them from their duty until the destination had been reached".

"Were they a kind of guard dog?" Bliss asked.

"Yes," answered Daisy, "They would prevent an attack from the rear, but in truth, they were really for show, a kind of extra to the already splendid livery. These days coach dogs only perform that duty to show people something of life among the aristocracy of yesteryears".

"Where do you do your poncing about behind these coaches then?"

asked Basher mockingly. "I suppose it's when the idle rich get together to talk about how wealthy they have become on the backs of the workers".

"Don't be so silly," said Polly to Basher. "People like Daisy's owners have always had wealth and the last thing they would do was boast about it".

"Who asked for your opinion?" snapped Chico Chihuahua (who by the way was one of Basher's lackeys). "You have some room to talk when it comes to tyranny; your ancestors were living in the lap of luxury while the guillotine was working overtime lopping the heads off innocent people".

"Listen to the kettle calling the frying pan black," said Storm. "What about the Alamo then, answer me that? Wasn't it your Mexican friends who did in Daniel Boone, Davy Crockett, Colonel Bill Travis and all those other brave men?"

"Oh for goodness sake," said Bliss. "you lot are beginning to sound like a bunch of half-drunken humans. You're enough to make a body cringe with embarrassment. Do go on and tell us more" Bliss requested of Daisy.

"Have you met any famous people while you have been doing your thing?" asked Herman Schnauzer who had been content to just sit quietly and listen to the arguments. (Well, being of German origin he didn't want to be accused of starting world War One or Two or even both.)

"Have you really met lots of famous people?" simpered Polly Poodle.

"As a matter of fact," said Daisy, "I have been in the company of some of the most famous people in the country, maybe even the whole wide world".

Poor Polly could hardly contain herself as she pleaded with Daisy to tell her more.

"Once," said Daisy, "I was actually presented to royalty! That was when my owners were awarded the first prize for the best turned-out coach and livery. All the top families were presented that day and some people were heard to say that it was my performance that swayed the judges, who, by the way, had a prominent member of the royals on their panel".

"That's nothing," rapped Basher Bates. "Once when my guv was voted barrow-boy of the year, we were given the freedom of the East End of London and we were treated like royalty! We got drunk and stayed drunk for at least a week. It might have been even longer."

"Yeah, you tell her, Bash," chirped Chico. "Put that in your pipe and smoke it, Spotty", added the minuscule Mexican.

"Pay no heed to those who know no better," said Polly Poodle.

"The freedom of the East End indeed, who would want such a thing? No one of any refinement, that's for sure," added Herman Schnauzer, who by now was getting bolder in the knowledge that Basher and the Mexican midget were well out-numbered.

Daisy continued to tell us about her life at Havalot House and the famous people she had met. Polly Poodle gasped every time a rich or famous name was mentioned, Basher and his minute mate made jibes at every opportunity and Bliss, as usual, was ever ready to keep the peace. Daisy told how some of her relations had actually been coach dogs for royalty itself – when her mum gave birth to her and her brothers and sisters, four of them were promised as presents to a certain family who are quite well-known for riding in horse-drawn coaches.

"Oh, get her!" cried Basher Bates. "Well I would have Miss Fancy Pants know that my great-great-great-great granddad belonged to royalty; he belonged to none other than 'Artful Arry Oskins and Emily Oskins who where Pearly King and Queen of London. They wus real royalty they wus, not like them what you ponce about with".

Jet, nearly a labrador

"That's telling you Miss Stuck-up", shouted the cheeky Chico.

"Oh be quiet you, before you shrink and disappear altogether," said Storm.

"That's it," said Bliss, "enough is enough, bedtime all of you".

It felt so good to be back with my friends that I really didn't feel at all sleepy. I just lay there thinking back on that evening and smiling to myself at the antics of Basher Bates and his efforts to do his guv'nor's social standing some credit. I thought to myself how frustrating for poor Polly Poodle that she would not be able to tell her mistress - who by all accounts really was the ultimate in social climbers - that she had met Daisy who had actually been presented to royalty, maybe even the Queen.

What about little Chico, and his hanging on every word of Basher, in an effort to seal a friendship with the bossy Bull Terrier!

Most of all I thought about how readily Bliss and Storm had welcomed me back into their lives knowing full well that I could only be a problem to them. How lucky I was to have such good faithful friends.

The next morning Bliss said that as this was the day when the bedding store was due to be re-stocked, it might be a good idea if I was to visit Connie Collie and Annie Alsatian. They would be glad to see me, said Bliss, and I could tell them that there was to be a get-together on Friday evening at Three-Tops.

Storm led the way to the secret way out and gave me the usual lecture on being careful. "Mind now and stick to the river bank and no short-cuts".

As I made my way along the side of the little river I forgot all about my recent brush with the authorities. The sound of the river was too much to resist and although the morning air was still quite chilly I just had to have a paddle. After a play about in the water, I made my way to where I could see a flock of sheep for I knew that Connie would not be far away. When I was within hearing distance of the sheep,

I could also hear Connie barking out her orders.

"Stay with the flock you silly little lamb, get yourself back over here you dozy old ram; you should know better. Come on Mrs Woolly-Head! Show a good example to the kids. Heavens above" she said as I made my way towards her, "Is that really you? Come here and tell me all about what you have been up to. I heard you had been arrested for trying to murder some chickens".

I told Connie what had happened and she said that she never really believed the rumour about the chickens anyway.

"Whatever are you going to do now?" she asked.

"I'm not sure," I answered, "but Bliss said that we should have a get-together on Friday night to try to find a solution to my problems.

"Will you come?" I asked.

"Certainly I will," answered Connie, "and I'm sure Annie will want to be there too."

"Have you had something to eat this morning?" she asked.

"Not yet," I answered, "but I am sure I will get some food at Annie's".

"If you want to, you can go down to old Sean's house where you will find some food near my kennel. Old Sally will be there and old Sean has gone to town for the morning, so there is no problem."

I told Connie that I would much rather help her with the sheep for a while before I made my way to Freshwater. After a couple of hours of sheep herding I was happy when Connie suggested a paddle in the cool river. I remember thinking how much I envied Connie and her way of life. Mind you, I wasn't totally convinced that I wanted to play nursemaid to a bunch of woolly-wonders.

"Tell me," said Connie, as though she had been reading my mind, "have you got any idea at all about what you would like to do with yourself."

Jet, nearly a labrador

I said I didn't really know, but as long as I was in the countryside and was allowed to run free I didn't mind what I had to do.

"There is always the chance that you might be lucky enough to get a job with a gamekeeper, but then again, there is the problem of you being only 'nearly a Labrador'."

"My mum was a Labrador," I said, "and I take after my mum".

"That's all very well," said Connie, "but try telling that to some people and they would just laugh at you. Seems to me," said the canny Collie, "that what you need is an owner who likes walking in the countryside and knows a bit about hunting and such things. And more importantly wants a pet who likes to hunt on a part-time basis while being a companion the rest of the time".

"That sounds good to me," I said, "but I'm going to be very lucky to get a deal like that, especially now that I have got myself a criminal record".

"Oh blow that," said Connie". "That was all a mistake and heaven knows you had no idea that there was a bunch of paranoid poultry on the other side of that wall when you were forced to jump it".

"I know that," I said, "but you try getting the boys-in-blue to understand. And who's going to give me the benefit of the doubt now that I have gone on-the-run again?"

"You are just a victim of circumstances," said Connie trying to console me. "And anyway you haven't exactly committed a really big crime, have you?" she said, quizzingly.

"Of course I haven't," I answered indignantly. "What do you take me for, some kind of hooligan who goes around causing havoc?".

"No, no, of course not," said Connie, "but you must admit you're barely seven months old and you have been in more hot water than a teaspoon".

"I had a lousy start," I told her, "and it wasn't my fault that I was only 'nearly a Labrador'".

"Well at least you have come to terms with the fact that you are not a candidate for the cover of Country Life, and Crufts is a no-no. That's a step in the right direction, so there is hope for you after all. Now then young man, isn't it time you made your way to Annie's; you'll just be in time to have some lunch with her, compliments of the Freshwater Restaurant. Now don't forget to tell Annie to call for me on Friday evening on her way to Three-Tops. Off you go now and be very careful and remember, no short cuts."

As I made my way to Freshwater, I found myself wondering about who my old man was and what he might have been. They say the apple doesn't fall far from the tree and considering the amount of trouble I had got myself into so far, I was beginning to think that the absent parent might well be a bit of a scoundrel - or even a right blackguard! How could a lady like my mum get herself mixed up with someone like that? Somehow, sometime I would find out, I promised myself.

When I arrived at Freshwater, Annie Alsatian was just about to do the rounds of the vegetable and fruit gardens.

"Oh my dear boy," exclaimed Annie. "I have been so worried about you; how are you? Are you hungry? Where have you come from? Are the police on your tail? When did you escape from the nick? Come, tell me all about it".

I couldn't get a word in edgewise as Annie fired question after question at me. When she slowed down I told her all about everything that had happened.

"Well now," said Annie, "This is a fine old kettle-of-fish and no mistake! Whatever is to become of you? I don't think that running away from Miss What's-Her-Name was a very good idea. In fact, I never did think that leaving your yuppie house was the brightest thing you could have done, but however, that's all in the past and what really matters now is what can be done in the future".

Annie asked how everyone was at Three-Tops and asked if I had called on Connie on my way to Freshwater. I said that everyone was fine and told her not to forget to call for Connie on Friday evening.

Jet, nearly a labrador

I was just starting to get one or two hunger pangs when the door to the restaurant kitchen opened and Annie's master appeared carrying a huge bowl of goodies. He made for the kennel; I got myself out of sight. Oh no I thought as the man put the bowl down, smiled, crossed his arms and stood there saying "C'mon now old girl, eat it all up now, let's see a clean bowl".

I thought for one terrible moment that the old boy was going to watch every single morsel disappearing down Annie's gullet, but at last he turned and headed back to his kitchen. Annie beckoned to me and believe me I didn't hesitate. I was tucking into the grub before you could say 'Holy Mackerel'. When I had done justice to the lovely goodies, Annie said that we could go for a ramble along the riverbank. I had never been to that part of the river before so it was all the more exciting. Annie knew all about the creatures that lived in and around the river.

"Aren't you going to ask me what I'm going to do with my life?" I asked her. "Everybody else does".

"All right," said Annie. "What are you going to do with your life, now that you mention it?"

I told her of my wish to stay in the countryside and how I loved the water. Annie said that those were the instincts of someone of my breed; she said that I must have inherited them from my mum.

"Maybe you are not just 'nearly a Labrador' after all," she told me, and that made me feel really good. "If only we could find a way to let humans know what we wanted to do with our lives" she said, "everything would be so much simpler and there would be much happier dogs in the world – and owners come to that. Now take the case of Binky Basenji and his owners; nicer people you couldn't wish to meet, but as dog owners, forget it."

"When Mr. and Mrs. Welloff decided to move to the country, they thought it would be a good idea to have a dog. Now, never having had a dog before, they didn't have much idea. Feeding, watering, walking and taking old Binky to the vet for a check-up was the extent of the

Welloffs' contribution to the relationship. Now with some breeds that would have been enough. Probably even in the case of some Basenjis, life with the Welloffs might well have been satisfactory. It just so happened that Binky Basenji had inherited more than just a touch of his ancestors' love of hunting, which was to prove somewhat of a strain on the relationship.

The Welloffs were a couple of business types who had done quite nicely for themselves during the property boom. No children and pots of money,; they were used to the best that life had to offer and when the best didn't fit the bill then there was always the extraordinary and that's where old Binky came into the equation. Well let's face it, there were not exactly packs of Basenjis roaming yuppiesville and while the regulars of the local yuppie watering hole (pub to you) had their well-bred Poodles, Pointers, Springers and Terriers, the Welloffs had Binky Basenji. There was no doubt that buying Binky did the trick for the Welloffs. He repaid the investment and then some. The fact that old Binky didn't bark was a constant topic for conversation when the Welloffs paid their regular visits to the local watering hole.

"'Oh my darling, how quaint, a non-barking dog! How absolutely spiffing, you clever old thing! Where on earth did you find such a treasure? Do tell more about your adorable acquisition".

Now this kind of old chat might be just the business in yuppie circles, but it did nothing to further Binky's chances of staking his claim among the canine members of his new community. Poor old Binky, how could he make the Welloffs understand that he had needs apart from food, water and a walk to the pub. What he wouldn't have given for a day's hunting, running across open country, crashing through a forest, mud up to his hocks and the odd plunge into a fast-flowing river. It wouldn't even matter if the prey got away. In fact, that would be quite acceptable. Binky had heard about how his ancestors had been great hunters in Africa and all he wanted to do was emulate them. Oh, he knew that he would never get to corner a lion or tree a leopard or a tiger and it was a certainty that he would never get to sit around a campfire at the end of a hard day's hunting, but all the same, he could even make do with chasing a rabbit down a hole or sending

Jet, nearly a labrador

a squirrel scampering up the nearest tree. Poor old Binky! Although he tried really hard to be the kind of pet that the Welloffs thought they had bought, he found it more and more difficult to pretend. True enough, the people from whom the Welloffs bought him told them that it was in the Basenji character to be keen, devoted, loyal, easy to train and domesticate and although they did mention that the Basenji was a very courageous breed, they failed to mention that it might just be possible that Binky might need to be given the opportunity to prove his courage at some point.

Binky got more and more frustrated and turned to a bit of naughtiness. Mr. Welloff's Christmas present from his mother, handmade fur slippers, got some rough treatment from our hero while the leopard skin shoulder wrap that Mrs Welloff bought with the proceeds from her first big money deal was left looking more like a mangey moggie than a proud beast of the wild. The fireside rug that was once running wild was reduced to shreds and thereafter anything that moved or didn't move became fair game or even big game. Needless to say, the relationship between owners and pet became more than just a bit tricky, especially when the threats and ultimatums started to fly. Mr. Welloff was all for bringing the relationship to an end, but Mrs. Welloff was having none of that. If those other people could make it work with their pets, then so could they, she told Mr. Welloff in no uncertain terms. How on earth could the self-assured, self-made, successful business dynamic duo face their neighbours if they were to give up their dog? Getting shut of old Binky would as sure as eggs are eggs be seen as a defeat, and no way was the female half of the Welloff team going to stand for that.

It was decided then, that Binky was going to school and no expense was going to be spared. If the school didn't work then there was always the psychiatrist's couch or even a frontal lobotomy. So off to school went old Binky. He was picked up every morning and brought back home in the evening. As it so happened, he quite enjoyed the new experience and meeting others like himself with problem owners gave him a chance to exchange notes on the subject. It soon became clear to him that this school was in existence to shape and mould pets to fit their owners' wishes and desires, irrespective of what the pet might want, or even need. All of the dogs at the school were said to be some sort of problem or other: some aggressive, some disobedient, some destructive and some just downright little vandals. After talking with some of the others, Binky was beginning to think that he was not really all that badly off as far as owners were concerned and, while the Welloffs might be a pair of wallies in some respects, they were kind and the digs were good. If only they would give him what he wanted: a couple of hours once a week doing his thing. Then there would be no more naughtiness.

It was while Binky was serving his time of corrective training that things started to happen that would change his life. Reports that a large cat which had escaped from a circus was seen in the area were confirmed when livestock was attacked on farms. It was thought that the animal had made itself at home in the area because of the nature of the surrounding countryside. Hunting for food at night, during the day there were literally hundreds of place the beast could lie-up: caves, old lairs, woods and even old mine shafts were in abundance, which made it very easy for the animal to evade capture. Teams of men and dogs were of no use, the barking dogs only served to alert the big cat before anyone could get near enough to fire a tranquillising dart into it.

It had been agreed that as the cat was only killing to eat, every effort would be made to capture it alive and return it to the circus. What was needed was a dog capable of finding it and getting in close without alerting it. Well now, if ever a dog was made for a job like this, it was Binky. Well, the hand of fate was at work and Binky and the big cat were about to become a part of each other's destiny. A team of big cat experts was brought in to help and one of these men just happened to have spent many many years in Africa. Fate was indeed conspiring as only fate can because when the Welloffs took Binky to the pub who should be there, but our intrepid tracker. The man had taken a room at the local watering hole. When he saw Binky Basenji, he could hardly believe his luck. The man told the Welloffs of his time in Africa and how he and other hunters used Basenjis to help them in their work.

Anyway, to cut a long story short, the Welloffs agreed to loan Binky to the tracker.

Jet, nearly a labrador

The very next morning, man and dog set out to find the big ca,t who by now had the local population scared out of their pants. From the moment they had met there seemed to be some kind of invisible link that created an immediate bond between man and dog. Maybe it was the fact that deep down they each yearned for the past: Harry, our tracker/hunter, for his years of excitement in Africa; and Binky for experience of life, as it must have been for his ancestors. After a few miles of walking, Harry sat down and lit his pipe and as he watched Binky he was sure that the Basenji knew exactly why they were there. How right he was, for every hunting instinct that Binky had ever felt was no longer simmering underneath, but brought to the surface by knowing that somewhere out there was a beast which he, Binky Basenji was going to hunt down and corner, just as his ancestors had done.

Binky was not the only one bristling with excitement; Harry too was feeling his blood coursing through his veins at the thought of the job in hand. As the two set off again, Harry spoke gently to Binky, every soft command obeyed and every request answered without hesitation. Before very long, the two were working as one and Binky's ability to second-guess Harry's every word and movement amazed the tracker. In all his years of hunting and tracking in Africa, there had only been one working dog who could do that with similar accuracy. How strange, thought Harry, we have only known each other a matter of hours and yet we seem to know each other's very thoughts.

Hour after hour went by and with each new hour came a heightened feeling of excitement as man and dog sensed that they were closing in on their prey. Harry wished that he knew more about the surrounding countryside, but what he lacked in local knowledge his instincts more than made up for. He also knew that his faith in Binky's hunting ability would be rewarded. Before very long Binky was showing Harry all the signs of a Basenji closing down on his prey and when the dog entered an old cave partly hidden by brush, Harry knew that the search was over. Binky placed himself at the mouth of the cave and if there had ever been the slightest doubt in Harry's mind about what was in there, well there was none now.

Harry took his radio transmitter from his backpack and within a short time help had arrived. Harry had told the other trackers to leave their dogs out of earshot for fear of spoofing the cat into making a break from the cave. When it had been established that there was indeed only one way in and out of the cave, it only remained to decide how to take the beast alive. Someone suggested that they bring up the other dogs and send them into the cave. Too messy, said Harry and all that frenzy would be sure to create panic on both sides and someone or something would be bound to get hurt, or worse.

Harry bent down to where Binky was still guarding the cave opening. He stroked the Basenji and spoke very softly. The words were gentle sounding, but only the two of them had any understanding of their meaning.

Jet, nearly a labrador

"What's he saying?" one man asked another. "No idea'" came the reply. "Sounds double Dutch to me," said another.

"Mumbo-jumbo," said another.

"Clear the brush away," Harry told the others. "And put the nets over the cave entrance".

When everything and everybody was in place, Harry lifted the net and whispered to Binky. Without a second's hesitation, the courageous little Basenji was on his way into what could have been the jaws of death. It was only a short time later that the cat was entangled in the net, a tranquilliser dart sticking from its rump. It was soon at peace and on its way home to the circus, or maybe a zoo, or even a wildlife reserve. Binky, without as much as a scratch on him, curled up at Harry's feet as the men celebrated their success over a few drinks. There was no denying who the hero of the hour was as the Welloffs bought everyone enough drinks to corner the beer market.

"What was that language you were speaking to the dog outside the cave?" one of Harry's mates asked him. "Sounded like Swahili or Dutch Afrikaans to me".

"Well now," said Harry. "I suppose you're not far wrong".

"What was the last thing you whispered to Binky before you sent him into the cave" asked someone else.

"Ah that," said Harry. "I told him that he, the cat and I were all Africans under our skins".

"What a terrific story," I told Annie. "Did Binky have to keep going to school?"

"Oh dear me no. The Welloffs, being the kind people that they were, decided that perhaps they and their lifestyle were not quite right for Binky Basenji. Harry was made a present of Binky and they spent many happy years roaming the countryside and any time there was something to be tracked down the authorities would send for Harry and Little Simba."

"Who was Little Simba?" I asked Annie.

"Oh dear, I forgot to tell you, Harry renamed Binky, saying that Binky was no name for a Basenji".

"What does Little Simba mean?" I asked Annie.

"Little Lion," said Annie, "Just like one of Harry's favourite hunting dogs from his years in Africa".

"Did Mr and Mrs Welloff buy another pet?"

"Oh indeed they did," said Annie, "a nice quiet little Toy Poodle which Mrs Welloff was often seen carrying rather than walking. Come on now" she added, "we must be making our way back to Freshwater".

When we got back we went into the vegetable garden so that Annie could do her rounds. I asked her why they didn't use scarecrows to frighten off the rabbits and birds.

"The owners did use scarecrows for a while," she told me, "but well, it didn't scare the rabbits and the birds got so used to seeing it that one of them started nest-building on its head".

Annie said that I should start out on my way back to Three-Tops before it started to get dark.

"Don't mess about now," she told me, "don't stop at Connie's and don't take any short-cuts and don't get into any more trouble".

As I made my way back to Three-Tops I couldn't help thinking about Binky Basenji, or should I say Little Simba. How lucky for him that he should meet someone like Harry the Hunter. Just imagine, if that animal had not escaped from the circus, things might have turned out very different indeed for old Binky. On the other hand, if Harry had not stayed at the Welloff's local watering-hole he would never have met Binky and who knows what sad end would have befallen the big cat. Most of all, the Welloffs would never have admitted that owning a

Jet, nearly a labrador

dog like Binky Basenji was just not on for them, and was so unfair for poor old Binky. Oh dear, I thought, how complicated life is. All the same I also thought that someone somewhere must have been looking out for old Binky, Harry, the big cat and even the Welloffs.

When I saw a rabbit dancing about in the middle of a field, I couldn't resist chasing it all the way back to its warren and when a squirrel jumped up in front of me, I pretended that the squirrel was a leopard and I was a famous hunter. I chased the squirrel until it ran up a big tree. As I looked up at the leopard (sorry, squirrel), I knew how a real hunting dog must feel as he waited for his master to catch up with him. It was while I was fantasising that I suddenly remembered what Annie had said about 'not messing about'. So I set off once again for Three-Tops. When I arrived there was Storm waiting by the secret entrance and looking like a worried father waiting for his late-home daughter. I thought I was in for a telling-off. Storm was as nice as pie, but just when I thought I was off the hook for being back late, Bliss appeared and gave yours truly the mother and father of a tongue-lashing.

"Will you never learn; how many times and how many of your betters is it going to take before you take any notice of what is being said to you? It's small wonder that you are in a mess with your life; all you had to do today was have a nice time with a couple of friends and come home at a reasonable time, but oh no not you; you had to drag it out until you had me worried out of my mind".

On and on went Bliss until Storm came to my rescue.

"Alright dear, alright, I think he might have got the message now," said Storm.

"Well I just hope so for his sake," said Bliss as she glared at me.

Storm said that it had been a very, very long time since he had seen Bliss as mad as that and I should go to the bedding store and not make a sound, at least until his sister had cooled down. I didn't need telling twice as I made for the store and sanctuary from Attila the Hen Bliss. I lay down in the nice fresh straw and before very long I was asleep. I don't know how long I had been in the land of nod, before I heard Bliss asking if I was hungry. I was absolutely starving, but I said (like you do when you're in the dog-house, so-to-speak), just a little. Bliss took me to the food and I did the business on it.

"There now," said Bliss "that will keep you going for a while," as she watched me lick the bowl clean.

Bliss said that I should go back to bed, but Storm said that I could go with him when he did his last round of the day.

While we were checking the perimeter fence, Storm said that Bliss was sorry for being so hard on me earlier, but he also said that I deserved it.

"You really must try harder," said Storm, as we did the round. "Bliss and I and Annie and Connie, well we sort of feel responsible for you in a way and we want you to be happy."

I told Storm that I did try, but somehow things always seemed to turn out wrong for me.

Jet, nearly a labrador

The next couple of days I spent mostly helping Connie Collie with her sheep and Annie Alsatian at Freshwater. I didn't sleep very well on Thursday night; I lay awake thinking of what was going to happen at Friday evening's get-together. After all, my whole future might depend on the outcome. All kinds of thoughts were coming and going through my head. A job with Connie and Old Sean, helping Annie at Freshwater or maybe I could join the Army. I knew the chances of becoming a police dog had gone when I got myself a criminal record. Maybe I could be a gamekeeper's dog; with my luck the chances were that I would more than likely be a poacher's dog.

Friday evening came and by the time Annie and Connie arrived at Three-Tops I was feeling all of a dither. Seeing old Sally had decided to invite herself along did nothing at all to put me at my ease. Lovely old girl that Sally was, rumour had it that when she retired from sheep herding, flocks of sheep all over the country celebrated for a week.

"Quiet please," said Storm, as the gathering talked amongst themselves. "Settle down now and we can make a start".

"You all know why we are here," said Bliss, "but for those who are in any doubt, I will explain again. Young Jet here needs our help to decide what might be best for his future. As you may or may not know, Jet was a Christmas present which for one reason or another just didn't work out. Now we all know many stories of Christmas and birthday presents that don't work out, but we are not going to get bogged down in the rights and wrongs of present giving in the shape of a pup. Young Jet is at a crossroads in his life and he needs all the help he can get, so if anyone has any suggestions, then please speak up."

"What would you like to do?" old Sally asked me.

I answered that as long as it allowed me to stay in the countryside I didn't mind very much what job I did.

"Well," said Sally, "that narrows it down to a few hundred options at least. The trouble with you youngsters today is lack of respect, not nearly enough discipline," said the old sage turning to Bliss.

"Here we go," said Basher Bates, "blame everything on the young. I suppose your generation did everything right and proper."

"Now, now," said Daisy Dalmatian in her best posh voice. "That is no way to speak to an old lady. You ought to be ashamed of yourself."

"Who asked for your opinion, Spotty?" chirped Chico Chihuahua, ever ready to suck up to Basher. "What would you know about life among us mere mortals."

Alzah the Afghan hound said that in his native land, someone in my predicament would simply go into the mountains and join up with a gang of bandits.

"We don't have gangs of bandits," said Connie Collie.

"Oh yes we do," said Basher, "only we know them as aristocrats and the like."

"That's not fair," whimpered Daisy Dalmatian. "My owners are kind, gentle people who would not take anything that wasn't theirs."

"I agree," said Basher. "The trouble is they believe they have a God-given right to everything."

"There now," said Padser the Irish Terrier, who by the way had just that day arrived at Three-Tops. "Put that in your pipe and smoke it Miss Bountiful, sure wasn't it the likes of your owners' ancestors that turfed, no pun intended," said Padser, as he winked at Basher, "the likes of my owners' ancestors out of their homes when they couldn't pay the rent because the potato crops failed."

"True enough," said MacBeth the Scottish Terrier. "Aye laddie, true enough and wasn't it the very same Sassenach blackguards that tried it on in the Highlands and Lowlands of my ain haime-land."

Poor old Daisy Dalmatian was distraught.

"Now, now," said Storm, "that's enough and anyway, none of that has got the least thing to do with Daisy or indeed what we are supposed to be discussing."

Jet, nearly a labrador

"It's all that Basher's fault," said Boris the Russian Borzoi. "He would cause trouble in an empty house."

"That will do," said Bliss in her fiercest voice. "I will have no more of this bickering."

Just then Chico Chihuahua said that Boris Borzoi had no room to talk considering the track record of some Russian aristocrats. Well, Bliss nearly hit the roof as she ordered the cheeky Chihuahua to his bed.

"Now," said Bliss "may we continue; is there any chance of finding Jet something to do at Freshwater?" Bliss asked Annie.

"Not really," answered Annie. "I only wish there were, but as you know there are times in the year when even I have to look for things to do."

"What about Old Sean?" Bliss asked Connie.

"I really don't see how we can take him in," interrupted Old Sally.

Basher Bates mumbled something, which the others luckily enough didn't hear. I think it was something about an old crone taking up good room. I'm not quite sure. Connie Collie said that she liked me very much and she told the others that I was good with the sheep and knew how to handle them, but all the same, they really didn't need another shepherd.

"Why can't Jet stay at Three-Tops?" suggested Daisy Dalmatian. "After all, he likes it here and he could share his time between here, Old Sean's and Freshwater."

"Well, not really," said Storm, "that was only a temporary arrangement and Jet needs a home of his own."

"What about Havalot House?" asked Paddy. "Sure begorrah, there must be any amount of work on an estate of that size for a young fella such as yer man there. Sure wouldn't he be a great help to your worship and your ladyship. Come to that, sure a little scamp like himself with knowledge of the criminal world would be worth his weight in pheasants to a gamekeeper plagued by poachers."

"That's a lovely idea," said Daisy, "but Havalot House has not escaped the pressure of market forces and already there are signs that cut-backs will be inevitable."

At which point Basher jumped on to his soapbox.

"Oh yeah mate, we all know what that means, don't we just? The workers, mate, that's who will be cut back; get two to do the work of ten and cut their pay and that's market forces for yer, my old mate."

Old Sally was asleep, thank goodness, when Padser asked Connie if the auld biddy was going to be replaced when she chased her last lamb, so to speak.

"That's not a very nice thing to say about poor old Sally," said Pang the Pekingese who had not as much as uttered a single word up to

that point. "We respect our elderly where I come from and we listen to what they have to say, because the elderly have wisdom. 'Confucius say - young man with fast mouth have tortoise for brain'."

"Is that right now," said Padser indignantly. "Well now, we look after our elderly and Con Murphy say 'Little fellas that butt into other people's business should be made to live with the rest of the fairies'."

Jet, nearly a labrador

Bliss, as usual, did her peacemaking bit and order was restored.

"Seems to me," said Storm "that Jet's best hope is to give himself up to the authorities and hope that someone adopts him. He might just get lucky and find a really good home. After all, none of us got to choose our owners anyway."

"That's true enough," said Annie "and if his next home doesn't come up to the mark, he can always have it away again."

"That's very well," said Basher, "but he just can't keep on having it on his toes for the rest of his natural."

"What do you think me auld darlin'," said Padser to the now wide-awake Sally, "the little Chinaman says that we should listen to your words of wisdom and right he may well be, for sure. As me auld ma used to say, 'shut your gob and listen when your elders are speaking'."

"Well," said Sally "I have lived a lot longer than most, and not all of my life has been a bed of roses. I have known good times, but one thing I can tell you is, you only get out of life what you are willing to put into it. It's just possible," said the old girl looking at me, "that you were a bit too hasty in running away from your first home. Maybe if you had worked a bit harder on your yuppie family you might have been able to turn a few things in your favour. Oh, I have no doubt that you had a cross to bear, but then, haven't we all? If it's not one thing with humans, it's another. Lord only knows they are not the most uncomplicated of species, and it's up to us to do what we need to do to simplify their lives. There again, I'm quite sure that you are very much a wiser young man for the experience, and I'm also sure that you will have learned a great deal by listening to the many friends you have made in your short life. Having said all that, I agree that the only sensible thing for you to do in the circumstances, is to surrender yourself to the authorities."

"Has anyone got anything to add to that?" Bliss asked. Nobody said a word, and the silence told yours truly that a decision had been reached.

"Would you like to say anything?" Storm asked me.

I said that I would like to thank everyone for being so kind to me.

"Don't be silly, me old china," said Basher, "that's what mates is for."

"Ah go on with yis," said Padser. "Sure wouldn't you yourself do as much for a body."

"Think nothing of it," said Daisy. "One must do what one can for one's chums."

"Ach, away wi ya mon," said MacBeth, "if ya canna di a gid turn ner di a badden."

"Maybe you will get the opportunity to help someone some day and if you do then that will be all the thanks we need," said wise old Sally.

Alzah and Boris both said that they had been glad to help. Annie said that I would always be welcome at the Freshwater Restaurant; Connie said the same applied at Old Sean's farm. Bliss and Storm said that I must never forget where they lived. It was agreed that I should spend

Jet, nearly a labrador

the weekend amongst my friends and give myself up first thing Monday morning. I had a smashing couple of days, running free between Three-Tops, Old Sean's farm and Freshwater Restaurant. The weekend went all too quickly.

Monday came and as agreed, I made my way back to the nick. The strange thing was that I felt really good as I waited to be captured. I didn't have very long to wait and soon I was being gone over to see if I had been injured in any way. They also checked me for fleas.

"Been walkabouts then have we?" asked one of the screws as he took me to my cell.

"Looks in very good trim for a vagrant," said another, while Miss Piggy said she was not amused. "You little monkey, you made a right wally of me, running off like that."

I looked as innocent as I could and hoped and prayed for mercy. Well, I did what I was told and tried my very best not to get into trouble, which for someone who is 'nearly a Labrador' *and* with a criminal record and from a one-parent family as well as with an identity and an attitude problem, was not easy.

Shortly after giving myself up, I was put on the 'Available to Good Homes' wing. That's where you go when the screws decide that you are fit for life outside the nick. It was only a matter of days before things took a turn for the better. A couple looking for a dog was being shown around and something told me that the woman would be just right for me; a piece of cake; putty in my paws. As for the bloke, well to tell the truth, I was not all that sure about him; not exactly your shifty type, more your 'do as you're told' type. It was when I heard the bloke tell one of the screws that he was looking for a dog he could train to hunt that my ears pricked up.

As soon as they got to my cell I put on my intelligent look and showed all the character of a kennel full of hunting dogs. The bloke stood looking at me for a while and then he asked the screw if he could take a closer look. Hello I thought, I'm in with a chance here. The woman just looked on and nodded every so often. It was very obvious that I was going to be a man's dog – which of course was fine by me.

"He'll do," said the man in an Irish accent.

The screw said that there were some things the man should know before making a final decision.

"He's got a bit of a history," he said.

"Sure haven't we all," said the man. "What's he in for?"

"Has trouble settling," answered the screw.

"He's not vicious is he?" the woman asked.

"Doesn't seem to be, but we don't really know a great deal about him."

Don't tell her about the chickens, I was thinking and don't say anything about running away from Miss Piggy. I needn't have worried, the screw made me look like a candidate for the Nobel Peace Prize.

Anyway, the man said I was far too young to be a real problem and besides, there was nothing that he and I couldn't work out between us if we tried.

My kind of man, I thought; my kind of man, firm but fair. A dog would know where he stood with an owner like that and such an owner would stand by his dog through thick and thin. It was settled then, I was going to live with the nice kind lady and the geezer with the funny Irish accent.

Oh no, I couldn't believe it, they lived in a flat! My new owners lived in a flat over a shop in the High Street! So much for my hopes of life among the country set, I thought, as I was taken up a steep flight of stairs. It didn't take me very long to discover that the front door was the only way in and the only way out and not as much as a single blade of grass was to be seen anywhere. It was hardly what I had in mind, so it was no wonder that I was already making plans for my escape. Things did pick up a little when the missus put my first meal

Jet, nearly a labrador

before me; a lovely meal it was, cooked to perfection and plenty of it followed by a bowl of cool milk from the fridge. It was obvious from that moment, where yours truly was going to do best in this set-up – if, of course, I decided to stay. I couldn't quite get an angle on the male half of the duo. Deep, he was deep, and then some. I was going to have my work cut out with him, I thought as I looked at His Highness.

The big meal was doing what big meals do and as we were in a flat I hoped that these two realised that sooner or later that very same big meal would appear in the open for the second time. No need to panic though, the Quare Fella looked at me and announced "C'mon now me auld Segocia, time for your first walk. Are you coming with us?" he asked the missus.

"Just give me a minute while I put the dinner in the oven," she answered.

Off we went on our first walk as a trio, or even a kind of family, I suppose. I must admit, I was just a little excited as the lead was put on me and we set off. It was only a very short time before we were in the middle of the most wonderful country: fields and hedgerows, rivers, ditches, crops of all kinds, rabbits, hares, squirrels, foxes and every game bird known to working dogs. This is it, I thought as I looked around me. Even if His Highness doesn't have a clue about my needs, I can do my own thing whenever I'm let loose. Maybe living in the flat with these two might work out after all. Might as well give it a go, I thought, as we walked along the edge of a wood.

I was to learn a lot about His Highness on our first walk as he told the missus about his plans for me. "By the time I've done with him, he'll be an all-round man's dog" he told her, who thank God pointed out to Rambo that I was still very young and needed tender handling.

It was at that very moment that I came to believe in the God of Dogs. Here I was with one owner who not only understood my needs, but was ready and willing to work on them with me and another owner to whom I could do the occasional bit of 'woe is me'

when I felt like a bit of spoiling. One thing I was sure about, by the time the walk was over, was that His Highness really did know a thing or two about us dogs, which meant that it was not going to be quite so easy to blind him with canine science. Still, I would cross that bridge when I came to it. After all, I was not exactly behind-the-door myself when it came to human-canine relationships. When we got back from our first walk, the man patted me on the head, saying "There now me auld darlin', sure now that wasn't too terrible now was it?"

The missus was far more to my liking, asking me if I was ready for something to eat. I hadn't given it much thought before, but it was when I settled down for the night that I realised something: 'No kids'. No tail pulling, no ear twisting and no finger poking in the eye. It was getting better by the minute and when the missus looked at me and pointed to the end of their bed giving me the okay to sleep there, well all thoughts of escape went out of the window. I can tell you, yours truly was staying and no mistake; just try getting rid of me I thought, as I lay on that bed all cosy and warm.

"You've landed on your feet here my old son," I said to myself. You may not have had the best start in the world, but you have certainly cracked it now."

The first week I felt like a bug under a microscope with His Lordship watching my every move. Getting to know the little fella, he told the missus. Mind you, I was also keeping tabs on him and his moods. Between you and me and the gatepost, His Majesty was getting over a very sticky patch in his life and I was to be part of the cure. Fresh air by the bucket load and long walks was to be the order of the day for the old reprobate, which of course suited yours truly down to the ground.

Now, by all accounts, His Eminence had been a bit of an artist, only not the kind of artist you associate with brushes, paints and canvas; more of your bottle, glass and tumbler-type artist, which told me that, for whatever reason, the old bog-trotter's life had not been all that very different from my own; not exactly a bed of roses. There were, no doubt, some who said that the old codger's problems were self-inflicted, but then, the very same thing could have been said of me. One thing was for sure, he looked like a man who had not had the best of times recently and still had a way to go. Talk about the blind leading the blind, there was I trying to learn all there was to know about hunting from a bloke who had problems just getting himself out through the door!

Apparently, if humans got themselves into the you-know-what through too much elbow bending at bars, then they were given treatment which included drugs. Now some of these drugs did funny things to some of these elbow-benders, just you ask me old guv'nor.

Anyway, I just thought I should tell you that bit of gossip. Not that anything the old fool did before I came along is any of my business.

So, off we set on our journey through life, the boss trying to get back on track and me trying to get over a poor start. I wouldn't say that we were an instant success as a team, what with me being more than just a little bit impetuous and the old rake going about like a bear with a sore head. I suppose we were made for each other in a way and you know what they say, 'God made them and the devil paired them', at least that's what my old mate Padser the Irish Terrier used to say about his owners.

Living in a flat became quite tolerable despite the lack of a bit of garden and there's no doubt the grub and the digs in general could not be faulted. A fine cook was the missus and the old reprobate boss really did know how to look after me.

Apparently, my guv'nor's old man was a bit of a dab hand with dogs and horses, so I suppose that's where he learned so much. Do you know, he could tell when I had a chill or a cold before I knew?

As we got to know and understand each other, the partnership blossomed, the guv'nor was growing in confidence and I was getting to be the kind of hunter that I always dreamed I would be. Don't get me wrong now; we were not a couple of bloodthirsty killers who set out every day to see how much wildlife we could decimate. Oh dear me no, it was the finding of the prey through tracking and the quartering of open land that gave us the buzz, as they say. I won't deny that we scared the living daylights out of many an unsuspecting rabbit, hare and pheasant!

I was one year old and according to the guv'nor, I was coming on like a house on fire, well at the old hunting game anyway, but in the flat, an absolute pain in the you-know-what. Shoes, slippers, loose mats or anything else that I could amuse myself with, got the treatment. I even chewed up a pack of two hundred cigarettes. I would have smoked them, but I couldn't find the old man's lighter! The trouble with me was that I had never been allowed to be a puppy for very long and as you well know, we all need to do certain things at certain times in our lives, so I was just doing those things that I should have done as a puppy.

As I have already said, my guv'nor was a dog's man and he understood me; the missus too was a brick during my barmy period. "Poor little mite" the missus would say, "we don't have any idea what he went through before we got him." Can you believe that? "That's all very well", the guv'nor would say, "but if we don't do something about it, the little mite will start eating the furniture and before we know it, the flat itself will be on the menu."

I seemed to find trouble where there was none. As my guv'nor used to say in the early days of our partnership "That dog would cause trouble in a monastery."

I remember the first time I went with them on the weekly shopping expedition. As usual, the boss was as enthusiastic about shopping as a turkey is about Christmas. The car journey was a thing to behold, the boss doing his best to look and sound like the dutiful spouse and the missus looking like the 'cat who got the cream' because she had managed to get the old reprobate to take her shopping. Anyway, when we arrived at the car park, the super-shopper boss told the missus that he would just walk me around for a couple of minutes, just in case the car journey had upset my tummy.

"You go on ahead now," he told the missus, "and sure I'll catch you up in a little while."

Jet, nearly a labrador

Off we went towards the river that ran through the park across the way from where the cars were parked. It was a hot day and the car journey had indeed got yours truly a bit hot'n'bothered, so the cool water looked more than a little bit inviting.

"Would you like a little paddle?" asked the boss, looking down at me.

I gave him one of those imploring looks that Labradors are famous for and almost immediately the lead was whipped off and the cool water was lapping about my feet. The boss sat down on the riverbank and lit a fag, the trauma of the shopping gone from his thoughts. His mind must have wandered. Some children, who had been playing further along the riverbank, were now playing with yours truly and before you could say 'breast-stroke', a ball was flung into the middle of the river and I was in pursuit. I should tell you at this point, that up till then I had only paddled in shallow water, so swimming was not something that I was familiar with. The ball seemed miles away as I flapped and floundered in my efforts to retrieve it. The children shouted and hollered in wild excitement and the boss (who had by then returned in mind to our planet) was on his feet and shouting instructions for me to "Come on out of that water you little gob..."

By this time there was more than just the odd shopper gathered. People were coming from all directions and the shouts and threats from the riverbank were getting louder by the second.

"If you don't get yourself out here this instant I will come in there myself and drag you out by the scruff of the neck," roared my guvnor.

The river was wide and deep and I was just not getting the hang of the swimming business at all. In fact, I must have been giving the onlookers a bit of a fright because panic was setting in on the riverbank.

"The poor little thing," said one woman. "He's drowning, someone get a rope!" shouted a concerned man.

"What's it doing in there anyway, if it can't swim?" asked another.

"Whom does it belong to?" inquired someone.

"That fellow there," said the mother of one of the kids who had chucked the ball into the water.

"Shouldn't have a dog if he can't look after it," said one bloke.

I might have been drowning, but I sure enough knew what was coming next.

"What's that you said?" barked the guv'nor. "I'll give you can't look after my dog. If you don't shut your gob, you'll be joining him in the river!"

"Is that so?" yelled the interfering bloke.

At that very second it was as though something or someone eased me to the bank and the boss yanked me out of the water. I was fully expecting a clip round the ear-hole or at least a real telling off, but the boss just stood looking at me saying "There now me auld darlin', sure isn't that grand, me doing the shopping and you learning to swim and all in the same morning."

The guv'nor stepped up his 'get back to normal programme' and I was more than a willing participant; mile upon mile of walks,

cross-country treks which sometimes kept us out all day long and
I was loving every minute of it. I was learning every trick in the bag
as far as hunting was concerned and quite frankly it was fast becoming
a very one-sided contest between the wildlife and us.

Now as you know, us Labradors and even 'nearly Labradors', are not
exactly ferocious and we don't go throwing our weight about; but all
the same, the guv'nor expected me to be ready to stand my ground in
a tight corner, especially when I was being picked on. Well, he had no
need to worry himself on the score, I had learned to look after myself
while I was on the run. If you are wondering why all this fighting
talk, then let me explain.

The guv'nor had been born in Ireland at a time when men were
men, the women were proud of it and a dog was not so much a pet,
more a provider. I know this because Padser the Irish Terrier told me
things that would make your hair stand on end. At the time the
guv'nor was growing up in Dublin, dog fighting, badger baiting and
many, many other forms of cruelty were rife. A sort of way of life, for
the so-called 'dog men' of that time. The thing was that it was all a
kind of pastime in some circles and the kids of that era accepted it all
as normal. I don't suppose they were cruel people really. According to
Padser, the going was mighty hard for most people and that was
reflected in their general outlook on life. Besides, there was precious
little to do in the way of pastimes.

Like I said, the guv'nor grew up among hard men and even harder
dogs, but between you and me, I don't believe that he was all that
happy in that environment. Don't get me wrong, he has never been
a shrinking violet, but I just don't believe that he was cut out for
watching cruelty.

The kids whose old fellas went in for blood sports had no say in the
matter, they did as they were told and even if they found blood sports
distasteful, well that was just too bad. I suppose in a way, my guv'nor
had very little choice, but to go with the flow, so to speak and anyway,
from what I could gather, disobedience was not an option in those
days, especially not in their house. The thing was that there were men

who saw nothing at all wrong with two dogs trying to duff each other up just to prove a point. The point being, which human nutter owned the nuttiest dog and believe it or not, some of the moronic mongrels actually enjoyed it, the dogs too. Well they do say that some dogs are mirrors of their masters. Mind you even in these times, there is a certain amount of cruelty amongst so-called 'dog men' and what makes this modern-day cruelty even more despicable is the fact that such things as dog fighting is motivated by financial gain. In the old days, a man who owned a real champion-fighting dog was given a lot of respect, irrespective of the man's status in everyday life. Don't get me wrong now, I hate and despise any form of animal cruelty, as does my guv'nor, and nothing in the world can justify dog-fighting, but I must tell you the story of Peg the English Bull Terrier and her owner.

Peg was born in London at the time of the Blitz, during World War Two. She was bought as a present for the father of a young Irish boy serving in the British Army and taken to his home in Dublin. From the very instant that Peg was introduced to Mick, an uncanny sort of bonding took place. Mick had owned many a champion dog in his time: fighting dogs, hunting dogs, show dogs and racing and coursing greyhounds, but none had ever got as close to him as Peg. Maybe it was because she had been a present from his eldest son and she represented a link between father and son while the boy was fighting in the war. Mick himself had done more than his fair share for King and Country during the First World War; wounded twice while fighting on the Somme he knew all too well the horror of war and what his sons were enduring.

Peg was fast becoming a perfect specimen of the English White Bull Terrier and it seemed only a matter of time before Mick's cronies would bring pressure on him to prove Peg in the fighting arena. Mick knew all about the world of dog fighting and much as he wanted to prove her courage, something deep down prevented him from putting his beloved Peg in the arena.

Mick decided that Peg would be a show dog and not a fighting dog and being no mean exponent in the art of fisticuffs himself, he got very little criticism from his cronies (well not to his face at least).

Jet, nearly a labrador

A powder-puff, a white lily, a lap dog, nice to look at, but not the real article were just some of the sayings attributed to Peg, but still Mick would not be shaken in his resolve not to let her fight. Mick knew what Peg was made of and in his mind she had nothing to prove. She had shown her courage that morning in Perry's fields when a bull attacked Mick and one of his younger sons. They had been out from early morning with a couple of Mick's friends and their Lurchers. Hunting rabbits was not only a favourite pastime, it also put a good meal on the table and the blackberries picked by the younger members of the hunting party also helped to fill a hole in empty tummies. Anyway, the men had decided to have a break from their hunting, so they sat on the riverbank and lit up their cigarettes. The talk was about that morning's hunting and as usual the conversation soon developed into tales of days gone by; stories of men and dogs the like of whom would never be seen again.

Like Darkie Finn and his courageous bitch Jess, who between them saved the lives of four children from drowning in Murphy's quarry. The kids had been using the quarry as an ice-rink when the ice broke. Darkie, who had been ratting (hunting rats) with Jess nearby heard the screams of the children, and without one second's hesitation, was taking off his clothes and plunging into the icy waters of Murphy's quarry. One child was grabbed by Darkie's outsized hand and another kid somehow managed to clutch the big man's shirt. Two saved and two to go thought Darkie, as he plunged into the quarry for the second time. He knew that every second was vital because of the extreme cold and that if he could repeat the first performance and get the two kids out in one go, then they would both have a chance. The weight of the clothes on the struggling kids was taking its toll and as Darkie reached them, one of them slipped below the surface. Darkie's mind went into turmoil as he tried to decide on his next move. Should he take a chance and go for the one below the surface first in the hope that the other child could keep struggling, or should he make sure of saving another young life? It was as though the big man was seeing everything in slow motion and that was something that Darkie had experienced once before in his life.

It was in the trenches during the First World War that a youthful Darkie Finn had to make his first life or death decision. An enemy grenade thrown into his trench was the occasion when he first found himself in a kind of slow-motion world. In that situation he saw no other option but to throw himself onto the grenade with only one thought in his mind: to save his comrades.

This was very different as Darkie decided to go underwater. He put his arm round the drowning child and as he came to the surface he couldn't believe his eyes. There was Jess, his powerful Kerry Blue Terrier, with her jaws locked into the clothing of the remaining survivor, thrashing her way towards the quarry's edge. With all four children safely in the warmth of Murphy's farmhouse, all Darkie could talk about was his Jess, and how until that very day she had been terrified of even a drop of water, let alone a freezing quarry.

News of Darkie and Jess's heroics soon spread far and wide and everywhere they went they were treated like celebrities. Every time Darkie called into a pub for a jar someone would put a pint into his hand. Darkie would often say how if that old grenade had not cost him an arm, then he could have had a pint pushed into both hands.

It must have been because everyone was so engrossed in the story telling that they failed to hear the shouts from the next field. Mick's young fella had been picking blackberries from a clump of bushes in the middle of the field when lo and behold what should appear, but a young bull! The lad being wise to the ways of the countryside knew better than to run from it, for even if the bull didn't mean any harm, it could still do a lot of damage if it decided to have a bit of fun with you.

When Mick and the others eventually heard the boy's shouts, they went to investigate. Something about the way the bull was acting told them that he was not simply looking for a bit of fun. The boy had somehow got himself into the centre of the clump of bushes, so there was no immediate danger. All the same, bulls could be very unpredictable and if he took it into his head to charge the boy, a few bushes would not be of much protection. The bull would have to be somehow lured away from the clump of bushes, far enough away for the boy to make a run for it.

Jet, nearly a labrador

Everything was tried, but the bull was not for moving. Snorting and stomping the ground menacingly, the beast never moved more than a few yards from where the now terrified boy was trapped. The men even risked their dogs by setting them on the bull, but the animal was determined. It was as though it had made up its mind that the boy would not escape his wrath. Mick decided that if the boy could not get out, then he would try to get to the boy. The others tried to keep the outraged bull occupied while Mick circled to a point which put the bushes between himself and it. Mick made his run from the edge of the field, but it was when he was in no-mans-land that the shape of the plan changed dramatically. Suddenly the bull was between father and son and there seemed little doubt as to which member of the family was in the greatest danger.

The sight of the bull suddenly appearing between himself and the boy had caused Mick to break his stride and he stumbled. The bull was now giving all its attention to the father, which at least gave the boy a chance to run for it. Prompted by the others, the boy made his dash to safety. In the meantime, the bull was closing in on Mick. It didn't charge, but moved slowly as it bellowed in a kind of triumph at the sight of its would-be victim. Mick knew that it was pointless to turn and run; he would never make it before the bull ran him down and gored him. Still the bull was content to move in slowly as though it was relishing the job in hand. Mick too, was using his head. He would take full advantage of the bull's decision to stalk him. Moving slowly backwards Mick would wait until the odds were more in his favour, and then he would make his life saving run. God willing he would make it to safety.

By this time the others had moved around the edge of the field to see what was happening. The sight of the others must have triggered something in the bull, the beast lowered its head and began to trot. Mick turned and began his run, his legs pumping for all they were worth; he could almost feel the heat from the bull's snorting nostrils. He was not going to make it, so he decided to throw himself to the ground and roll to one side, which just might foil the charge. It was in the instant that Mick hit the ground that he saw what looked like a white flash going over his head. Rolling to one side and springing to his feet Mick realised that what he had seen was Peg in full flight launching her muscular frame at the bull's head. "Run for it Mick!", shouted one of the others, "Run for it!"

Peg's master heard the shouts and he knew that he should indeed 'run for it', but how could he desert his beloved courageous friend in her fight against a foe so much bigger and stronger than her? After all, she had not deserted him in his need. By this time the bull was more concerned about the pain in his nose, as the bitch tightened her vice-like grip. High up in the air went the bull's head in an attempt to shake off the white demon and when that didn't work he flung himself to the ground, the powerful neck jerking the head in all directions. But even that did not make Peg release her hold.

Mick shouted at Peg to "let go girl, let go!".

Still she hung on. Realising that there was not really anything he could do, Mick went to join the others in the safety of the hedgerow at the perimeter of the field. Lo'n'behold, as soon as her master

Jet, nearly a labrador

reached safety, Peg released her grip on the bull. Mick called Peg to come to him, but she just stood looking at the bull, as though she was scolding the beast for having the temerity to attack her master. The poor bull looked relieved to be free of the white demon, and the look in its eyes was more reminiscent of a bewildered sheep than an outraged bull.

The beast properly chastised, Peg made her way to the hedgerow with a dignified gait, as only one of her breed could. Mick never did give way to the pressure from the world of cruel sports. In fact, the men who had witnessed events that morning in Perry's fields were affected by Peg's display of courage and loyalty and that was the beginning of the end of dog-fighting, and some other kinds of blood-sports. Mind you, hunting rabbits continued, as long as empty bellies needed to be filled.

Life in the flat with my guv'nor and the missus took on a very different shape when he felt confident enough to find himself a job. No more seven hour cross-country treks and no more leaving the flat just as dawn was breaking, but even so, I was never left short of exercise. The guv'nor took on a job, which saw him working shifts, and it was some time before I could say with any certainty what time of the day or night we would go for our walks. The springs and summers were O.K., but for someone like yours truly living in a flat is not to be recommended. So think on, if you live in an upstairs flat with no access to a garden, and you must have a pet, get yourself a goldfish or a budgie. Now don't you go thinking that I am whinging about my time in our flat, I'm not, but oh boy, was I glad when I heard the guv'nor and the missus talking about buying a house with a garden. But that was a fair way off.

In the meantime, I was making loads of friends whose masters liked to do a bit of not-so-serious hunting. Well I suppose chasing a few rabbits would be a more realistic description of what we did. The competition was fierce between the dog-men to try and prove whose dog was best. Honestly, you just would not believe it! As for us dogs, well we just did enough to humour the humans. Throughout history men have always wanted their dogs to be the best at whatever they did; hunting, fighting, retrieving, racing, coursing or even just being a companion and housedog who could be trusted around children. There's nothing wrong with that and being good at something has its own rewards for us dogs, but some humans don't quite know or understand too much about the world of dogs. Consequently things do go just a little wrong from time to time between what an owner expects from his dog and what the dog is willing or even capable of delivering. Men trying to improve on nature have been the curse of the canine community for as long as humans have claimed dogs to be their 'best friends'.

Let me give you one example of men meddling with dogs and Mother Nature and getting it awfully wrong. The idea of the offspring from a match between a Greyhound and a Bull Terrier was too much to resist for a couple of old timers. The speed of the Hound and the courage, ferocity and stamina of the Bull Terrier would surely produce a litter of pups such as the hunting world had never seen before! In theory, that should have been the case. However, the reality was quite different. The offspring from the odd pairing were quite useless. The pups inherited their Bull Terrier mother's love of just lying about and sleeping at the drop of a hat and her hatred of exercise of any description. On the other hand, they inherited some of their father's speed, but he also passed onto them his terrible fear of water, his soft streak for all things smaller than himself, his aversion to violence and his love of humans. Mind you, they made the most wonderful household pets you could wish for. After the guv'nor had been back in work for a while, they decided to buy a new car, well not a new, new car, if you know what I mean, but a good car all the same and very comfortable it was too. Weekly trips to the seaside were a real treat for all of us and swimming in the sea became one of my favourite activities. The guv'nor, too, enjoyed a dip so that made it all the better.

I remember one time that things got a bit dodgy. The guv'nor must have been in an adventurous mood as he told the missus to keep me with her.

"I'm going a bit further out than usual," he told her, "you keep him with you until I shout to you to let him come to me".

Jet, nearly a labrador

Off went our would-be-channel-swimmer and the further he went the more concerned I became. Now my guv is not a silly man, but like all humans he is prone to the odd moment of pure unadulterated stupidity and this looked like being one of those moments because, firstly the tide was coming in and secondly, he could just about keep himself afloat in the water. A dolphin he is not. Anyway, I couldn't just sit there and watch while the old half-wit drowned himself and besides I didn't want to have to break in a new master. I was just getting this one somewhere near the mark. I struggled free of my lead and into the sea I went. The missus was shouting her head off and waving her arms about trying to get the old man's attention. I found swimming against the tide to be very hard going indeed and I was beginning to understand why the guv'nor had left me with the missus in the first place. As the incoming waves lifted me I could see him. He was making

straight for me, which was just as well, because by this time I had swallowed more than just a drop of salt water. The guv was doing his demented leprechaun bit.

"Get yourself back to the beach you stupid little gob...!", he roared at me. "In the name of all that's holy, what do I have to do to get you to do as you are told"?

I was too far out to swim back and I was taking on more water than the Titanic, so I made one desperate effort to reach my manic master. Just in time, I reached him and I suppose I saw him as a kind of island, because I planted myself firmly on his back.

"Holy Mother!", he screamed. "You'll drown the so-and-so pair of us!" He reached back and grabbed me by the scruff of my neck, but by this time I was in a panic and no mistake. When we got back to the safety of the beach, he gave me the mother and father of a telling off. When he realised that in my blind panic I had made a load of scratch marks on his back, well, he just went mental altogether. Now I don't know if you have ever seen an Irishman throwing a wobbler, so all I can tell you is, it's a sight to behold. As usual, the missus came to the rescue and after a nice cup of tea and a fag, things got better. However, I became very good in the sea and learned how to use the waves to my advantage. I made sure that I would never be embarrassed again over a drop of water even if that drop of water was the North Sea.

Talking of things embarrassing always reminds me of Fergal Foxhound. Now Fergal was one of a litter born to a mother who was part of a pack of hounds belonging to a very famous hunt in Ireland. When Fergal was just a pup, he had an accident, which left him with a gammy leg, and it was agreed by those who knew about such things, that he would never be a member of the famous hunt. A Foxhound who had a gammy leg was not a thing to be, and if it had not been for Noreen, the wife of a kennel-hand, who knows what might have become of poor old Fergal. Noreen and Fergal became great pals and they were rarely apart. Noreen was a gentle, kind woman and some people said that it was her love and care for Fergal that cured his gammy leg. Fergal was scarcely a year old when the gammy leg was no longer gammy and he was as sound as any one of the famous pack. In fact, he was such a fine looking Foxhound that Noreen's husband suggested that Fergal should rejoin the pack. Noreen would not hear of such a thing; Fergal was her dog and that was that and besides, she did not want him killing other animals. Needless to say, Noreen's husband didn't press the point and anyway, Noreen's gentle nature and her love for Fergal had probably turned him into a wimp making him quite useless as a Foxhound.

Jet, nearly a labrador

Noreen had been born and brought up in the city and what she knew about country life she had learned since marrying. She had never really given much thought to the rights and wrongs of foxhunting and anyway, her husband did make his living from the hunt, so she could hardly voice an opinion contrary to the practice, but she was sure of herself when it came to Fergal. He would not be part of the hunt. Far from being that, Fergal would be seen running behind Noreen's bicycle on her visits to the village and even carrying a newspaper or some other article in his mouth. Although Noreen got on very well with the villagers, that did not stop some local wags from making fun of the city girl and her so-called Foxhound. Calls of 'tally ho' and the occasional blast on a hunting horn could be heard whenever Noreen biked to the village with Fergal in tow and although Noreen ignored such behaviour, her husband was embarrassed by it.

Fergal blossomed into the most perfect specimen of a Foxhound and although he was dedicated to his loving mistress, he couldn't help wondering what it would feel like to run with a pack of hounds. Noreen too began to wonder if she was doing the right thing by her companion. After all, he was bred to run with the pack and hunting was in his blood from way back.

Noreen's husband was convinced that Fergal was becoming restless, especially on days when the pack could be heard running across the countryside. The baying of the pack and the shrill of the hunting horn would arouse his instincts and more and more Fergal longed to be a part of the hunt. He was becoming a very mixed-up Foxhound and much as he loved Noreen, he knew that he must run with the pack, at least once. So it was decided, the next time the hunt took to the field, Fergal would join them.

On hunt days, Noreen would usually visit her parents in the city as her husband would be out all day and Fergal knew that although their garden was surrounded by a high wall, he could still get out.

The day of the hunt came. Noreen went to visit her parents and Fergal waited to hear the sound of the pack. The moment arrived and Fergal cleared the garden wall as though it didn't exist. His heart beat faster as he closed on the pack. At last he was running with the hunt and his head was spinning with excitement. All the pent-up feelings and frustration of the past eighteen months were forgotten as he barked and bayed with delight. At last he was doing what he was born to do. At first the other hounds paid no notice, but when he went to the head of the pack he was scolded by one of the senior members.

"Where do you think you are going?" demanded one of them, "and what's more where have you come from?"

Fergal explained that he had once been part of the pack, but had been injured and rendered unfit for service.

"Oh dear," said another, "Are you the one they call the 'bicycle hound'?"

"The 'paper boy'," laughed another.

Poor old Fergal was taking a right old ribbing, but one of the seniors said that at least he was here now and that meant that Fergal had not entirely forgotten that he was born a Foxhound.

Jet, nearly a labrador

"C'mon now," said one of the others. "Give the young fella a break. It's not his fault that he is molly-coddled, and he is trying."

"Alright now," said one of the very senior hounds, "Enough of all this waffling, there's a job to be done. You there," he said to Fergal, "get back to the rear with the rest of the youngsters, and be quick about it."

Fergal soon realised that there was more to foxhunting than just running wild across the countryside. Apart from a pecking order, there were all kinds of rules and regulations and there were people to enforce them. Still and all, he was running with the pack, and enjoying every minute of it. " A bit different from running behind Noreen's bike" said one of the pack to Fergal, as the hunt raced across open land, leaped walls and hedgerows, crashed through the undergrowth, slurped through mud and negotiated fast-flowing rivers. Yes indeed, thought Fergal, and wasn't it exciting. Time and again Fergal raced to the head of the pack, only to be scolded by a senior and told to slow down.

Eventually one of the pack explained to him that it only became a kind of free-for-all-race when a fox had been sighted and the hunt was in full flight.

"What's it like living in a house with a family?" one of the young hounds asked.

"Oh it's alright," answered Fergal. "Very comfortable, and you get lots and lots of tit-bits of all kinds of food."

"That sounds good," said one of the others. "But do you not miss the company of the pack?"

"Well", said Fergal, "I was only very young when I had my accident, so I can't really remember what life was like in the kennels." "I would love to live in a house with a family where I was the only pet," said Felicity, one of the young female Foxhounds. "I would be ever so good and I would run behind my mistress's bike and I would carry the newspaper in my mouth and I wouldn't care a jot what other silly dogs or their silly owners said about me."

"How do you know what I do?" Fergal asked Felicity.

"Oh my dear Fergal," said Felicity. "You and your mistress were the talk of the countryside for weeks on end, and your Noreen's husband was the butt of many a joke among the kennel-hands."

"Oh dear," said Fergal, "No wonder Noreen's hubby was so anxious for me to rejoin the pack."

"Well," said Felicity, "I suppose we Foxhounds are meant to chase foxes rather than bicycles."

"Have you ever killed a fox?" Fergal asked Felicity.

"Oh dear me no," she answered. "I leave that sort of thing to the bully-boys. Besides I don't know of any fox who has ever done me wrong. What about you?" asked Felicity "Would you kill a fox?"

"Oh no," answered Fergal. "I couldn't, and besides, heaven knows what it would do to my gentle mistress if I did kill other animals."

Fergal asked Felicity if there were other members of the pack who felt the same way. Felicity said that many of the females and some of the young males just simply took part in the hunt because they had to.

"What else can we do? We have to at least go through the motions or we would very soon be out of a job, to say nothing of a home, and we might not all be as lucky as you in finding someone like Noreen."

It was about then that things started to happen. It was obvious even to a beginner like Fergal that a fox had broken cover and was running for its life. Someone shouted 'tally ho!' and a hunting horn sounded. All of a sudden, men, women, horses and hounds were instilled with a kind of frenzy. The excitement reached fever pitch. People shouted, dogs barked and horses flared at the nostrils as the hunt picked up momentum. Fergal could not help but be affected by the moment. He just wished that the chase could end by means other than the demise of the fox, which it so often did. Just then Felicity made her way alongside Fergal.

"Follow me," she said, as she veered away from the pack.

Jet, nearly a labrador

They were going through some very heavy undergrowth and with all the excitement going on, nobody noticed the two of them leaving.

"Where are we going?" asked Fergal.

"Never mind," said Felicity. "Just follow me."

Felicity was running like the wind and it was all that Fergal could do to keep up with her. When they emerged from the undergrowth they were well ahead of the main pack, and had the fox in their sights. Somehow Felicity found the strength to go even faster and Fergal barked at the terrified animal to go-to-ground, go-to-ground. "We won't harm you." The fox being something of a 'Doubting Thomas', was not quite ready to believe a couple of blood-thirsty Foxhounds, but being a clever animal he also knew that he could not go on running for ever. And anyway, the two hounds looked as though they were capable of catching him if they had wanted to.

Out of sight of the hunters and the main pack, the fox went to ground. Felicity and Fergal changed direction slightly and soon the hunters were chasing an imaginary fox. Slowly but surely, Felicity slowed the pace, and when they reached a small wood she brought the whole proceedings to a kind of dishevelled gathering of people, horses and hounds. The fox must be here somewhere, said one of the huntsmen; spread out and search. And search they did, but to no avail, for as Felicity and Fergal and some of the young hounds knew, Mr. Fox was probably sitting down to tea with his family and telling them all about his very strange experience. It had been a very hard chase and as the hunt made its weary way home, Fergal told Felicity how he had enjoyed his first day in the field, and how he couldn't wait for the next one.

Felicity told Fergal to be sure to go into the river and wash all the mud from his coat and she made him promise not to breathe a word of what he had seen. Cross my heart and hope to die, I won't tell a soul. Tell me," said Fergal, "do you do what you did today every time the hunt goes out?" "Oh dear me no," answered Felicity, "we take turns. Next time my sister Fenella Foxhound will be responsible for seeing to it that there is no bloodshed."

That was the story of Fergal Foxhound as told to me by a certain Trail Hound, who, by the way, assured me that he was a direct descendent of the said Fergal and a lady Foxhound who just might well have been the lovely Felicity. Now as you know, Trail Hounds are used in the sport of following a scent that has been laid along a planned route, and does not involve bloodletting in any way, shape or form. Sport without cruelty, you might say, which of course is what Fergal, Felicity, Fenella and their young friends were all about. I will leave it to you to decide whether or not a certain Trail Hound was the teller of tall tales or not. As for me, well, I believe every single word of it, but then, I'm just an old romantic at heart anyway.

I overheard the missus talking to the boss the other day, and what I heard has cheered me up no end. Apparently, we are about to look for a house with a garden; something that will be most welcomed by yours truly. I haven't been down in the dumps or anything like that, but since His Grace started back to work, my countryside recreation time has taken a bit of a pounding, to say the least. In fact, it would be fair to say that my roaming in the gloaming has been drastically reduced. However, if the extra money speeds up the process of moving to this house with a garden, then who am I to complain? Weekly trips to the seaside are the in thing at the moment and long may they last. I love swimming in the sea, especially when the tide is coming in. I swim out, ducking under the waves and when I'm far enough out to give poor old Tom a bit of a fright so he starts shouting his head off, I turn side-on and the waves carry me back; a bit like surfing really, only without the surf-board. A nice walk along the beach and a game of ball, something to eat and drink, a short rest, then back into the sea for another belly-full of salt water. A walk along the cliff tops, which is always good for a giggle, especially when I go just close enough to the edge for poor old Tom to have another fit of hysteria. After the missus dries me off and I look really grateful, we head towards the fish'n'chip shop, a move that is always very welcome after a hard day on the beach. After giving the fish'n'chips a respectful seeing off, a nice gentle stroll along the seafront as we make our way back to the car. Heaven, absolute heaven!

Anyway, life went on much as usual, and the only real change came with the house hunting. Now I'll let you in on a secret. Much as old

Jet, nearly a labrador

Tom wanted to move out of the flat and into a house with a garden, he knew in his heart that the time was not quite right, as far as house prices were concerned. Now I'm not suggesting for one minute that the old reprobate was some sort of a finance wizard. Far from it. In fact, if it was not for the money management skills of the missus, a cardboard box in a shop doorway would be more likely than a house with a garden, but it just so happened that he had been paying more than just a passing interest in the state of things in the housing market. Good thing too and fair play to the old boy. Otherwise, we might just have ended up in negative equity. Now, if you're wondering what someone who is only "nearly a Labrador" knows about negative equity, well, the answer to that is, quite a lot. The trouble with most of you humans is that you would never stop to think how something like negative equity could affect man's best friend.

Come to think of it, there are many situations and events which have a profound affect on our lives. Hatched, matched and dispatched (births, marriages and deaths to you) and even the first day at school are just some of the things that bring about feelings of joy, sadness, trauma or even depression for you humans, but try to remember, man's best friend has feelings too and can be just as much affected by life's rich tapestry of events.

To help you understand, let me give you some examples of what I mean. When Lydia left the nest to set up home on her own, her parents thought it would be a good idea if she had a companion, so they presented her with a three-month old Border Collie. Lydia named her new friend "Charlie" and they hit it off straight away, especially since Lydia was the outdoor type and as any Collie will tell you, an out-door type owner is worth their weight in gold. For a whole year the two were inseparable, but then quite suddenly, Charlie found himself spending a lot of time on his lonesome. Now poor little Charlie was, unlike yours truly, not very street-wise, so it took a while for the penny to drop, but drop it did. Exactly: the lovely Lydia had only gone and got herself another friend, a boy-friend no less, and without as much as a by-your-leave or a beg-your-pardon from poor old Chas (I called him that for short - anyway, he didn't like to be called Charlie).

Needless to say, the poor little fellow was devastated and when Rodders (Rodney the boyfriend) was invited back for coffee one night, poor old Chas was beside himself with jealousy. Things didn't get any better when the rotter Rodney had the audacity to sit in my mate's special chair and pat him on the head, saying, there now old chap, you don't mind if I sit here, do you? As time passed, Chas realised that he was going to have to play second fiddle to Rodney, but for all that, he knew deep down that Lydia had not stopped loving him and he was just glad to be around her. He told himself that it was just one of those things that happens in the lives of humans and to be honest, Rodney was not such a bad sort and there was the occasional walk, even if it was, only to the pub. Anyway, to cut a long painful story short, Romeo and Juliet (as Chas called them) tied the knot and before you could say "perambulator" there it was, a baby, another wedge driven into the gap between Chas and his beloved Lydia, and one more opponent in the fight for her love and affection.

However, things have a strange way of working themselves out, and mostly for the better if you just have a little faith, (as my old Daddy would have said, if I had ever known him,) which is just as well, because just as Chas was beginning to think that he was becoming surplus to requirements in the love nest, things did indeed take a turn for the better. Now, good old Rodders, although being a loving hubby and a doting Daddy had a very low thresh-hold when it came to screaming babies and it just so happened that the son-in-heir could have screamed for Britain and come away with gold every time. So how did that change things for the better? Well now, let me tell you. Whenever junior was about to give a performance, Rodney came under orders to take the dog for a long walk and Chas was obliged to tag along, as of course was only right and proper. After all, walks and dogs go hand in hand, you might say. Chas and Rodney were slowly but surely becoming more and more friendly and well, it was so much nicer for Rodney to walk in the fields and listen to the birds making a gentle sound rather than to listen to junior trying to outdo Pavarotti in the high note stakes. Rodders became a kind of born-again dog handler and it wasn't long before the whole family was going on long walks, that was when Chas was not looking after

Jet, nearly a labrador

junior in the garden while Lydia got on with the household chores and good old Rodney brought home the bacon.

Everything comes to him or her who waits, as the Missus has just found out. Our resident Chancellor of the Exchequer has just announced that the time is right, financially speaking that is, to do some serious house hunting. The Missus is over the moon and so is himself, but him being a man, he plays the strong silent part while she tells the world and his wife. As for me, well, I would love a house with a garden, but I'm just a little concerned. When Wally Whippet moved to a house with a garden, things took a turn for the worse, for poor old Wally, that is. His owner went all house proud, even to the extent that Wally got a room of his own. Well, more a house of his own. Well, a kennel really, in the garden. When an owner gets house-proud, it can have dire consequences for man's best friend, especially one who likes to get a bit muddy whilst playing with his mates or chasing some silly rabbit across a muddy field. When Wally lived in a flat, he was taken for a walk at least once a day, and sometimes two, or even three times, but since they acquired the posh house with a garden, well, the long walks tapered off to the occasional ten minute gentle stroll. There was the odd occasion when Wally was taken on a proper walk and I would get to have a chat with him, but these were few and far between and in the meanwhile Wally had become a changed dog, and no mistake. Once, on one of these few and far between occasions, I suggested to Wally that we should go and find a rabbit to chase, but he said better not, he might get all muddy, and the Missus would not be best pleased with him.

Now, having a female for an owner is all very well, and they are gentler and more loving than your average male, but they don't always appreciate that some dogs are bred for certain pursuits, like frightening the daylights out of rabbits and hares. The male of the human species is more in tune with that sort of thing. I suppose it goes back to when he was the hunter and had to provide the food. Mind you, they still do that to some extent, even if it is from the supermarket. Anyway, it seemed to me that something had to be done about poor old Wally and his predicament, but what? Maybe if Wally's owner (a single lady)

could somehow be paired up with a partner who was fond of the outdoor life, then a kind of normality might be brought about for the little fellow. Worth a try and no mistake I thought and I knew just the man for the job. Jake's master, that's who; he was a single male and he loved the outdoors. Jake was a Jack Russell Terrier who was a dab hand at finding rabbits, even when they didn't want to be found. The only trouble was that when old Jake put a rabbit to flight, that was the end of the hunt, for as you well know, a Jack Russell's little legs are no match for the speed of a rabbit who thinks the Devil himself is after it. But suppose Wally and Jake were partners, oh what fun they could have together! What a wonderful partnership I thought, and what a wonderful life they could have! And all I had to do was to pair-up their owners.

The very next time I met up with Jake, I asked him if he knew Wally Whippet. He said that he had seen Wally about, but not very often. I explained to him that since moving to a house with a garden, Wally doesn't get around much any more. Jake did nothing for my own peace of mind when he informed me that such things are not uncommon.

"You see," said Jake, "some owners seem to think that a garden and the very occasional ramble is all that any dog needs to stay happy." Now little Jake, being a bit of a wag, looked at me with an impish grin and reminded me that I too was about to move to a house with a garden.

"That's right," I answered, "but my Tom is a proper dog man and he knows what makes me tick." Under my breath I added, "please God." I told Jake all about my plan to bring his master and Wally's missus together and he agreed to help.

It really wasn't going to be very difficult to put the first phase of the plan into action and when the opportunity presented itself, Jake grabbed it with both hands, or in his case, all fours.

"Isn't he a little love!" said Wally's mistress, as Jake did his sweeter than candy act. "Well now," answered Jake's master, "you must be special, he is not usually as friendly as that with strangers." Which of course was the truth, for if anything, Jake was a stand-offish, independent no-nonsense dog, if ever there was one. Henry (Jake's master) had never known Jake to be so affectionate towards anyone before, not even to him, so it was no wonder that he found himself thinking that maybe this lady was indeed special. After a few pleasantries had been exchanged, the two parties went their separate ways, but little Jake knew that the seeds had been sown.

Several encounters later, as Henry and Jake were out rambling, Jake saw Jane (Wally's mistress) in the distance and his agile, cunning brain went into overdrive. Quick as a flash he was into the hedgerow making like he was in hot pursuit of a rabbit. Within seconds he had slipped away to where Jane and Wally were walking.

"Hello," said Jane as he approached, "where have you come from?" And before you could say "Yuk!" he was all over her like a rash. "Are you on your own, where's Henry?" Jane asked, as she scanned the countryside. Hello thought Jake, it's Henry is it, won't be long now before things start to happen. In the meanwhile, Henry was becoming worried. Jake was nowhere to be seen or even heard and it was not like him to stray too far from his owner. The clever Jake had every-thing under control, and when he knew they were in earshot of Henry, he began to bark as loud as he could. Poor old Wally didn't have a clue about what was going on, nevertheless, as he wasn't doing anything in particular, he thought he might as well join in the barking game. Before very long, Henry had made his way to the source of the noise and without even a word to Jake, he smiled at Jane and said what a lovely surprise it was to see her. Jane too seemed happy to see Henry, and for the first time, the two ambled along as though they were a couple, if you know what I mean.

The time had come to put Wally in the picture, so Jake explained everything to the wistful Whippet, who incidentally thought the plan to be a wonderful idea.

"Now then," Jake told Wally, "I'm going to flush out a rabbit from the undergrowth and you are going to chase the nice little bunny. You

don't have to catch it, you just have to chase it." Jake went to work and soon there was a rabbit streaking across the open countryside with Wally in hot pursuit. The sight was too much for Henry, and try as he did, he could not contain his excitement.

"Go on Wally," he shouted, "go on boy!" Jane too got caught up in the heat of the chase, and soon the pair of them were in harmony, offering encouragement to Wally. When the chase was over and the rabbit had gone to ground, Jane, slightly flushed, apologised to Henry saying that she was not really blood-thirsty, it was just that she had never before seen Wally in that way. Henry said that there was no need to apologise, he was certain that she was far too kind and gentle to be bloodthirsty, and anyway, the rabbit was unharmed and after all, Wally was just doing what comes naturally to him. A dog like Wally needs to do at least some of the things it was originally bred to do, Henry pointed out to Jane, and as there was no Whippet racing in the area, then the odd rabbit chase now and again would do nicely, if of course that were possible. Jane explained to Henry that having bought a new house recently, she was working longer hours to help pay for it and just didn't have the time to give to Wally.

Jet, nearly a labrador

"Oh," said Henry, "I hadn't realised that you were on your own". He went on to explain to her that he too was on his own, he was a writer and did most of his work in the evening or even sometimes through the night, which of course meant that he had considerable time free during the day.

It was some weeks and several meetings later that Henry plucked up enough courage to suggest to Jane, that if it were possible, he and Jake would love to take Wally on their daytime rambles with them. Jane said that she was sure Wally would love that and she agreed whole-heartedly. Jake and Wally became the best of pals and the pair made a formidable team of hunters (only for fun of course), which went down a treat with old Henry. Jane too was turned into something of a new woman. It was some time later that I bumped into Jake and asked him

"How are you lot getting on these days?"

"Like a house on fire," Jake replied "Well you have to, don't you, when you all live under the same roof."

Things are definitely on the move as far as a house with a garden is concerned. The Missus has started to scan the houses-for-sale pages of the local newspapers, and the guv'nor is up for it too. A few phone calls by the Missus and before you can say 'removal van' we are being bombarded by mail from every estate agent and his wife. House after house is looked at, and its good points and bad points discussed at great length. After a while it becomes a kind of hobby for the Missus and a pain in the 'you know what' for poor old Tom and yours truly.

Anyway, to cut a long story short, we eventually went to look at this particular house and straight away, I felt that this was somewhere I would like to live. A Hail Mary and three Our Fathers later and bobs your uncle, the Missus, being the intelligent woman she is, was also declaring her love for the newfound home. Mind you, as soon as I saw the huge kitchen, I knew straight away the Missus would be in favour, as she likes to do a lot of cooking and as old Tom says, when she cooks she needs a lot of space. A garden where I could lie out in the sunshine was my preference, and this one fitted the bill very nicely. There was just one little worry about the new abode and I must admit I did feel more than just a bit concerned at first. The new house was on the opposite side of the town to where Tom and I did most of our rambling, and thoughts of Wally and owners moving into new houses with gardens started the odd little alarm bell quietly ringing. But surely not? No, never in the world would good old Tom make his bestest mate live in a kennel in the garden. What an absurd notion I told myself, as I raised my eyes to Heaven in a silent prayer.

I was a little sad as we left the flat to take up residence in our new home. Somehow I sensed that my days of roaming across the countryside playing the hunter were numbered. I would miss that very dearly. I would also miss my daily chats with my many cronies who I had shared many a yarn with, to say nothing of the odd 'tall story' that would creep in from time to time. I found consolation in telling myself that, well, maybe it was high time that I stopped frightening the living daylights out of the wildlife population, and besides, I was no spring chicken after all. In truth, I had been feeling the odd twinge here and there in the old limbs, to say nothing of a creak here and there in the weary joints, especially after a long ramble. Well now, twinges and creaks and all, I must admit that when old Tom looked at me and said, "C'mon me old mate, let's take a look at the scenery hereabouts," for a moment I felt like a two year old in the head at least.

It was a lovely day as we left for our first ramble from our new home and somehow I felt very contented, all things considered. I had no idea what to expect, but within a minute or so I was looking at a very pleasant sight: wide open spaces with meadowland, trees, hedgerows a beautiful winding river, play areas for the little toddlers and acres of space for the sporting types. I remember thinking to myself, well now, if a body has to retire, then you could hardly do better than what I was looking at. I was to be proved right about the retirement bit for as soon as we got back home, Tom told the Missus that he was sure yours truly would love it now that I was going to take things easy. It felt strange at first going for a walk with no real purpose to it, a kind

Jet, nearly a labrador

of gentle stroll, being absolutely respectable and bidding the time of day to all and sundry. Oh dear, I thought, this is going to take some getting used to. After all, I was more familiar with the nuttier types whose sole purpose in life was creating havoc with anything that moved and with hardly ever the time to notice the time of day, let alone bid it to anyone. Well, if it was going to be good enough for old Tom then it was going to be jolly well good enough for me. Well, at least, that's what I kept telling myself. Holy smoke, and me, a gentleman, what on earth would some of the old lags I met along the way have thought of that? I know exactly what some of them would have thought, and believe me, even I would not repeat their thoughts.

It took me longer than I thought it would to adjust to the slower pace of life, and getting to know what was acceptable and what was not took just as long. Whenever I did forget myself and put one of the more stroppy locals in their place, old Tom would explain to the owners that I had been used to the wilder side of life (whatever that was supposed to mean.) Most people understood, at least they said they did which was more than could be said for their canine counterparts. Talk about snooty, you would not believe the behaviour of some of the so-called toffs I was expected to make friends with. Blackguard, scoundrel, poacher, assassin were just some of the names attributed to me when the gossip started about how I had been a hunter of poor defenceless wild animals. But to be fair, there were those, humans and canines, who were most polite to old Tom and me, and even went out of their way to be nice to us.

Things were working out pretty well at the new house and they got even better when we had three children come to stay with us for Christmas. Life took on a whole new meaning that first time the kids came to stay. The smell of roast turkey wafting through the house, presents being opened with such gusto that even I had to bark with excitement, joy and laughter on so many faces (including the Missus and old Tom) just made me feel so good. School holidays and just about any opportunity brought the hustle and bustle that only kids having fun can create, and I loved every minute of it. So did the Missus and old Tom. Walks galore, picnics, blackberry picking, a lie down in a cool stream and all that followed in the evening by cuddles galore; at times I thought I had died and gone to Heaven.

I had enjoyed my life to date and there was very little I would have changed, but this new way of living was something else and what made it so complete was that it suited me down to the ground. Perhaps I had been living a lie, maybe I was the soft gentle type after all, and not the 'macho' mutt that I portrayed for so many years. A bit like someone else I know, and I don't mean of the canine variety.

I'm getting quite old now. In fact, if I were a human (God forbid) I would have had a telegram from you-know-who, quite some time ago. I can't get around very well anymore, so Tom and the Missus lift me into the car, so I still get to go to the riverside, and, would you believe it, the seaside. In fact, I had a little swim in the sea just the other day - not bad eh, for an old un? I suppose if I said I was getting weary, you would understand, but then again, you might not.

What I'm trying to say is that I believe my journey through this life is just about over, and what's more, my old mate Tom knows it too, (never could fool him all the time). But being the Christian that he now is, he knows that when this journey ends, another one begins, even for someone who is only 'NEARLY A LABRADOR.'

On October 17th 1996 at 3:30 in the afternoon, Jet ended his journey through life. He had spent the day lying in the bright autumn sunshine, with his head gently resting on Tom's lap.